Human
Resources

Also by Floyd Kemske

The Virtual Boss

Lifetime Employment

Human Resources

Floyd Kemske

NICHOLAS BREALEY
PUBLISHING

LONDON

First published in Great Britain by
Nicholas Brealey Publishing Limited in 1996
21 Bloomsbury Way
London WC1A 2TH

© Floyd Kemske 1995, 1996
The rights of Floyd Kemske to be identified as the author of
this work have been asserted in accordance with the
Copyright, Designs and Patents Act 1988.

ISBN 1-85788-114-1

British Library Cataloguing in Publication Data
A catalogue record for this book is available from the British
Library.

Printed in Finland by Werner Söderström Oy

To Rob,
patient guide
sympathetic friend
implacable taskmaster

ONE

BUT FOR the dry cleaning, Norman could have avoided being present when Blankenship shot himself.

The dry cleaning had apparently been ready for thirty days or so, because the dry cleaner called on Thursday to say he was getting ready to mark it as unclaimed. Norman had picked up the dry cleaning last time, but Gwen was putting in too many hours at the office these days to take her turn. Norman promised to go out at lunchtime and get it. Marriage isn't just about trading turns. Sometimes you put in extra effort.

He was walking across the company parking lot when he heard a loud cracking sound. He looked around to see where the noise had come from, and he saw Blankenship's car — a boxy sedan of economical design like so many of the company's scientists drove. Blankenship was an Assistant Manager in the Production Department and one of eight people scheduled to be fired that morning.

The driver's window of Blankenship's car was covered with red paint, and Norman wondered why Blankenship, who was ordinarily a pretty conventional person, would have painted his windows red.

Norman went to see, and as he got closer to the car he realized the red on the window wasn't paint. It was fresh blood. Very fresh. He ran the last few steps to the car and yanked open the driver's-side door. Blankenship was sitting straight up in the seat. His right hand lay beside him on the seat, with a pistol in it. His left hand grasped a chain, of the type used for Army identification tags. He looked like he was wearing a red skull cap of some sort.

But when Norman looked closer, he realized it wasn't a skull cap; it was, in fact, a place where there was neither cap nor skull, but a large opening. There was blood on the upholstery of the car, as well as some messy substance Norman did not want to investigate. It looked like he had shot himself through the roof of the mouth.

Blankenship apparently hadn't taken the time to study brain anatomy and had missed the important parts when he took his shot. He was still breathing. It was a bubbling wheeze, but it was breathing. Norman wished he'd not come out into the parking lot when he did. Blankenship's eyes rolled toward him.

Perhaps he'd managed to destroy his speech center because, although he looked straight at Norman, he didn't say anything. Norman wanted to run away, but he didn't. He just stood there and looked into the man's eyes. Blankenship's eyes rolled downward to the left hand holding the chain that hung around his neck. Then he looked back up at Norman.

Norman knew something was expected of him. He wanted to comfort Blankenship, but he didn't know what to say or how to touch him. He supposed he should tell him he was going to be all right, but the man had a smoking pistol in his hand and demonstrably preferred not to be all right.

As Norman stood there trying to decide what to do, Blankenship looked down at his chain again, then back at Norman.

Norman understood then that Blankenship was telling him to look at the chain. The man was plainly dying, and Norman did not want to touch him, even though he was lucid enough to know that Blankenship's problem could hardly be contagious. He forced himself to reach toward Blankenship's left hand, and as he did so the hand dropped away, revealing a trinket on the chain. It was a dull metal cross about an inch by an inch-and-a-half — a cheap bit of cast pewter.

Norman touched it. He looked back at Blankenship's face, but the man's eyes were no longer focusing. He had stopped breathing. Norman put his hand full on Blankenship's chest, and he felt a delicate fluttering there, then nothing.

He gently took the little cross and raised it until he could pull the chain, which was fairly long, up over Blankenship's head. The chain dragged across the top of his head, and some of the beads took some blood with them, so they looked as if they had been dipped in fingernail polish. He knew Blankenship had meant for him to have the cross. Norman was neither a religious nor a spiritual person, but he felt he had shared a major life moment with Blankenship. It was a profound experience, and he needed to commemorate it somehow.

He went back into the building to ask the guard in the lobby to call an ambulance.

Norman couldn't help but feel a little guilty about Blankenship. He hadn't been the one to lay him off, of course. That was Pressman's job. But Norman was the Manager of Human Resources, and he had processed the redundancy notice. He remembered being surprised that they were having a reduction in force. He thought the company was doing better than that. Did Blankenship know he had processed that letter?

He managed to retrieve Gwen's dry cleaning on the way home that night. He didn't want to have to tell her about Blankenship. It was Friday night, and he didn't want to spoil the weekend. But it might as well have been Monday, because Gwen said she had to go into the office for a few hours the next morning. It turned out she was too keyed up thinking about that to have sex that night. Norman would have liked to have sex. He thought it might have gotten his mind off what had happened.

Saturday night, Gwen was still worked up, and then on

Sunday morning, she read about Blankenship in the newspaper. The kids had already finished breakfast and were off watching television.

"You didn't tell me about this man Blankenship." Gwen looked up and folded the paper in her lap.

Norman reached for a bagel half and began to spread it with low-fat cream cheese. "I didn't think there was much to tell."

She looked at him and then unfolded the paper and resumed reading. They didn't talk about Blankenship again, but Norman thought she was probably thinking about it, because that night they didn't have sex.

They didn't have sex on Monday night or Tuesday night, either. On Wednesday night, Norman went into the bathroom to take Blankenship's cross from around his neck and put it in his pants pocket before going into the bedroom to undress. When he came into the bedroom, Gwen was brushing her hair in the mirror.

He walked over to the bed, and he remembered Pressman had scheduled him for an early meeting the next day.

"Would you please fix the children's breakfasts in the morning?" Norman folded the coverlet down on his side of the bed, pulled on the sheet, and doubled it over. He couldn't stand coverlet against his face while he slept. "I have an early appointment with Pressman."

"Again?" Gwen put down her hairbrush, slipped out of her nightgown, and climbed into her side of the bed without folding the sheet over.

Norman had early morning appointments with Pressman once a quarter, and it annoyed him that Gwen was surprised every time it happened.

"Yes." Norman suppressed his irritation. "He wants me there at five-thirty."

He took off his underwear and laid it on the chair, then switched off the lamp and climbed into bed. Norman and

Gwen had been sleeping naked for twelve years, and just because they didn't have sex every night seemed no reason to change the habit.

"Five-thirty? And you told him you would be there?"

"Of course." Norman rolled on his side to face her, and even in the dark he could see she was giving him that look.

"They'll never consider you for leadership in that company if you take orders from a jerk like Pressman." Her voice was quiet in the darkness.

"I don't take orders from Pressman." Norman sometimes felt he would never be able to get her to understand the situation. "It's the only time we both have open. We're on the same team, Gwen."

"That's insane," she said. "You're the Manager of Human Resources."

In one of life's little ironies, Norman and Gwen had almost exactly the same position in their respective companies. For Gwen, however, it was a leadership position. The company CEO sought her advice. Many of the line managers asked her input in their planning. She was a star at her company, and the word "team" did not seem to be in her vocabulary.

"It's just a budget review." Norman turned over on his back.

"Oh, Norman. You are so naive."

Norman hardly heard her. He was thinking about Blankenship again. Why hadn't he died instantly? Norman knew nothing about brain structure, but he thought it must have been a chance in a million for the bullet to find a path from the roof of his mouth to the top of his head without killing him instantly. Norman wondered if he'd been in pain as he sat in his car waiting for the damage to overwhelm his body and shut down his consciousness.

The room was silent, and Norman realized it was his

turn to say something.

"Can you fix the kids' breakfasts or not?"

"I have to be in early myself tomorrow." Gwen's voice drifted to him in the darkness. "I have to prepare for my weekend meeting."

"What's the difference between a weekend meeting and a meeting at five-thirty?" asked Norman.

"The difference is I choose to go to the weekend meeting. I haven't been ordered to be there by some troglodyte in Finance. I have important ideas to present there."

There it was again. Ideas. Gwen was apparently a fountain of ideas at work.

Norman wasn't exactly sure what these ideas were, but he knew from her conversation that Gwen had lots of them and that the people in her company prized her for it. Ideas seemed to be a fundamental part of the leadership she was so anxious he be considered for.

But Norman was more interested in successful teamwork than he was in leadership. He'd never had an idea in his life, but neither had he felt the lack.

"Do you have to be at the office before five-thirty tomorrow?" he said.

"No."

"I do," said Norman. "I win. Please make the kids' breakfasts."

"All right."

Norman felt the bed give as Gwen rolled over and faced away from him. He knew he had won too easily.

He could hear her breathing, and he wondered if they would ever talk about Blankenship. He supposed if they did, it would dredge up much deeper issues about who they were and what they wanted from life, issues they probably weren't ready to discuss yet. Would she say Blankenship was a loser? Would she be appalled that Norman had taken a cross from around his neck as he died?

It seemed to Norman that he was awake all night with

such questions, but when he heard his radio whispering soft rock music at him, he realized he had been asleep. He wondered when it had happened. He felt tired, but he switched the radio off and pushed himself out of bed before he could think about it.

He got himself ready for work while everybody else in the house slept.

Norman felt hurried — hurried and tired — when he found himself alone in the elevator at the office building.

Biomethods, Inc. had 1,000 employees, about a quarter of whom were scientists, and it made its money licensing its genetic discoveries to pharmaceutical companies. Norman understood nothing of these discoveries, but he took pride in the knowledge that his company was working on a cure for AIDS.

It was Norman's job to reconcile the company's Human Resources policies with Federal employment guidelines and to manage the people who administered benefits, orientation, and nontechnical training.

Norman liked his job and he was good at it, and he liked doing it in a company whose mission let him believe he was making a contribution to civilization. Two months before, he'd attended an empowerment seminar where the instructor had the participants — as part of an exercise to build self-esteem — write their own epitaphs. Norman struggled over the assignment for some time and finally came up with "Here lies the man who supervised the person who processed the salary increase requested by the manager of the person who discovered a cure for AIDS." He had been pleased with it, and when he got home from the seminar he'd told Gwen about it.

She had laughed. "That should be worth a directorship, shouldn't it?"

With Gwen, everything seemed to get back to advancement.

Norman yawned as the elevator chime sounded to

signal arrival at the Finance Department. Some things were more important than advancement.

The elevator door slid open into a corridor as dark as the heart of a Chief Financial Officer. Norman stepped out of the elevator and into a slot of light on the floor, which vanished when the elevator door shut behind him. The luminous face of his wristwatch said it was five-thirty. Outside, the sun wouldn't even come up for another hour or so. He'd had predawn meetings with Pressman more often than he cared to remember, but he had never learned where to find the light switch. He certainly couldn't rely on Pressman to turn on the lights. Pressman was in Finance and would rather risk his neck wandering in the dark than spend the company's money on lighting the hallway.

He knew he should wait until his eyes adjusted to the darkness, but the CFO expected him at half past five. Norman wasn't the only person who had early morning meetings with Pressman. As far as he knew, Pressman was at work by five every day.

Pressman had forty of these predawn budget meetings a year: one a quarter for each of the ten staff department managers. Norman didn't particularly like Pressman, but he respected that kind of commitment.

Biomethods, Inc. was divided into line functions and staff functions. There were five line departments: Finance, Marketing & Licensing, Cancer, AIDS, and Arthritis. (The latter three were named after the diseases most likely to generate profits from the company's biotechnology research.) And there were ten staff departments: Corporate Communications, Human Resources, Maintenance, Shipping & Receiving, Security, Administration, Safety, Information Systems, Community Relations, and Strategic Planning. Norman knew the names of the fifteen departments by heart. They were printed on boxes in the organization chart he kept tacked up on the wall beside his desk. He took a certain amount of pride in his understanding of the intricacies of the Biomethods organizational structure. It had been no small feat to master it.

The desk in front of Pressman's office was empty. It was one thing to demand that managers show up for work before the rest of the world was awake, but you couldn't ask such things of support staff. Norman skirted the desk and tapped on the office door, then stood there feeling the knot of his necktie with his fingertips to see if he could tell whether it was straight. He really couldn't tell by feel.

The door opened slowly into darkness, and a soft voice came from the office beyond it.

"Come in, Norman."

Norman stepped hesitantly into the gloom. He expected to find someone pulling on the other side of the door but, when he stepped inside, there was no one there. The room was dark except for a pool of white light on Pressman's desk provided by a halogen desk lamp.

He could make out a figure sitting on the other side of Pressman's desk, just outside the pool of light. The figure reached across the desk to pick up a wooden pencil. It was a man. His head and shoulders passed briefly into the pool of light, and Norman hardly had time to form any impression, but he could see the man was not Pressman. He was not anyone he had ever seen before.

"Come in, Norman," the man repeated. He appeared to be writing a memo with a pencil, which Norman thought a little strange. But when Norman looked closer, he saw the man was not writing but drawing, making a hasty sketch of what appeared to be a human face.

From Norman's perspective, the man's paper was upside-down and across the desk. Norman began to tilt his head to try to see what the face was supposed to look like, but the man opened his desk drawer and slid the paper into it. He then stood up from the desk lamp's circle of light into the darkness. "It's nothing," he said. "A habit I picked up from a boss I had long ago."

Norman did not understand. A habit of drawing pictures?

The man walked from behind the desk.

Norman's palms began to sweat when he saw that he was short. He didn't know who this man was, but experience had taught him to fear managers under five-six, and he estimated this one at five-five.

He could barely make out the man gesturing toward the sitting area at the other side of the enormous office. Norman was acutely aware he'd neither received an introduction nor been approached for a handshake. He walked to the sofa, set his budget report carefully on the coffee table, and sat down.

The man picked up another sheet of paper from the desk and carried it with him when he came over.

Norman wondered if he was going to sketch again.

The man switched on the lamp that rested on the end table next to the sofa, and its soft, yellowish light allowed Norman to get his first good look at the stranger.

This one obviously cared about his appearance. He had the even apricot coloring of someone who owns a tanning booth but is intelligent enough to use it sparingly. He was of indeterminate age, although his skin appeared unlined. A full head of white hair was slicked into place like a close-fitting crash helmet. He wore a pale pink shirt and a deep scarlet necktie. There was something very foreign about the man. His suit was a rich black with a subtle gray stripe and had the Italianate drapery of Louis, Boston. Norman and the other managers were trained to the boxy American look of Brooks Brothers.

The man pushed Norman's budget report aside and sat down on the coffee table facing him, still holding his piece of paper. Norman had never seen anyone sit on this coffee table before, and he was a little surprised at the ease with which the man carried it off. The two men were about eighteen inches apart, and Norman felt uncomfortable.

The man had still not offered to shake hands, and Norman wondered if this was some sort of intimidation strategy. If so, it was working. The man's eyes were impenetrable, but his face appeared relaxed and an engaging smile revealed teeth as even and white as if he'd bought them with an American Express Platinum Card.

"My name is Pierce," said the man. "Your meeting with Pressman has been called off — permanently."

Norman detected a faint soapy smell and concluded it was this man's breath. He didn't know what to say about Pressman's absence. He shifted himself on the sofa, uneasy at the man's proximity.

But the man seemed relaxed, and he spoke softly and evenly. "I don't think it's necessary to bring you in here every quarter and hector you about your budget performance."

"Are you the new CFO, Mr. Pierce?" Norman managed.

"Just call me Pierce, Norman." He leaned forward another few inches and studied Norman.

Norman remembered a high school biology class in which he'd been required to study a frog with similar intensity — after he'd eviscerated it. He smiled sheepishly, but he didn't move. He didn't want to offend Pierce by moving away while the man examined him. Norman was wary of offending short people, and frankly, remembering the frog, he thought this examination wasn't too bad. Time moved as slowly as afternoon traffic.

The telephone chirped, and Pierce's eyes flickered toward his desk. When he looked away, Norman found himself breathing for what seemed to be the first time since he'd entered the office. He reached up and felt the knot of his necktie. The telephone chirped again, then stopped.

"No." Pierce looked down at the paper he was holding. "I'm the new everything."

The two of them were so close that, even after leaning back away from him, Norman could see that the paper he was looking at was blank. Norman smiled and tried to laugh at Pierce's joke, but succeeded in producing only a nervous hiss. He wasn't used to people above him making jokes, and he was not a little worried for having found himself at the mercy of a man who drew sketches, sat on coffee tables, and studied blank papers.

"You'll be reporting to me from now on." Pierce continued to study his paper for a moment, then finally looked up. He didn't say anything else, and after an awkward moment Norman understood it was all right for him to ask questions.

"What—" Norman's voice came out dry and rasping. He interrupted himself, cleared his throat quietly, and started again. "What happened to Mr. Pressman?"

"Pressman's gone. So is the rest of the executive staff. They don't fit in with our plans."

An image flashed through Norman's mind. He saw Pressman and the rest of the directors and vice presidents, all dressed in dark Brooks Brothers suits, being marched out the front door.

"Ah." Norman wished he had something more profound to say than "ah," but there was nothing else to say. He couldn't risk revealing himself by asking the only question that mattered.

The man made a slightly sour face. "They hadn't an idea among them."

Norman was surprised. He'd always thought the executive team must have a lot of ideas.

"Have you ever heard the term 're-engineering,' Norman?" Pierce gestured with his paper.

Of course Norman had heard the term. He might not have any of his own, but that didn't mean he was oblivious to the ideas that occasionally gripped the business world with the intensity of a religious revival.

"No," said Norman.

Pierce turned the paper up and held its blank surface in plain view before him. "This is the company's new organization chart."

Norman thought it must be another joke. "Where's Human Resources?"

"There is no more Human Resources." Pierce's soft voice had the edge of a machete clearing away organizational underbrush. "There is no more anything. We're starting over from scratch with this company."

Norman wondered what was supposed to happen to the employees in a case like this. "There are some pretty good people here," he said cautiously.

"There may be." Pierce seemed unperturbed by Norman's caution. "But they are working in a dysfunctional organization. Let me ask you something, Norman."

Norman shifted himself on the sofa.

"What's the best thing about working for this company?"

Norman thought for a moment. He wondered what answer Pierce considered the right one. "The AIDS project," he said at last.

Pierce studied him. "AIDS is a pretty big problem, isn't it?"

Norman nodded, pleased he'd gotten the right answer.

"Is it a big enough problem to keep this company in business?"

Norman wondered what he meant by that.

"Tell me, Norman," Pierce said softly. "Do you know how many chickens there are in this country?"

Norman was uncomfortable. He wondered what chickens had to do with anything.

"Something over six point four billion," said Pierce.

"I don't understand," said Norman.

"Chickens have as many health problems as human beings," said Pierce.

Norman wasn't certain, but he thought Pierce's tone when he said the phrase "human beings" was a little disparaging.

"If a company is marketing a product of interest to a few million individuals when there is a market of six point four billion going unserved, don't you think that company might want to rethink its customer base?"

"What does that have to do with AIDS?" Norman tried to make his voice sound respectful.

"It has nothing to do with AIDS," said Pierce. "I'm just trying to give you some insight into why the venture group hired me to turn this company around."

Norman wasn't aware the company needed turning around.

"Never mind," said Pierce. "We'll go over these issues as time goes by."

Norman hoped the conversation would shift to something he could understand.

"I feel terrible about this man Blankenship," said Pierce. "I don't think the termination was justified, either. The other seven people will be brought back to resume work today. I want to start over on a new footing with the employees here."

Norman was surprised at how quickly Pierce shifted his conversation around. He tried to concentrate on everything the man said. He knew he must keep his wits about him if he was to hold on to his job.

"Norman," said Pierce gently, "the employees of this company are on the verge of hysteria. That a man would commit suicide because he got laid off shows a distorted set of priorities, don't you think?"

Norman was taken aback. What an ugly way to discuss poor Blankenship. He didn't know what to say.

Pierce seemed to take his silence for agreement.

"Good. I'm glad we agree. I'm going to need people like you to get this place turned around. I know the previous management wanted people to marry their jobs. This strikes me as some kind of primitive desire for mastery over others. I am not that primitive. We don't need devotion, just effective job performance."

Norman tried to figure out if anyone would think he had married his job. Did coming to five-thirty meetings constitute marriage to your job?

"What do you want me to do?" Norman's stomach growled from his lack of breakfast, and he shifted uncomfortably.

Pierce didn't seem to notice his stomach growling. "I want you to help me find the people that are at risk," he said. "People like Blankenship. The ones with leadership potential. The ones with all the ideas."

Norman was impressed with the man's concern.

"You and I, Norman, aren't the kind of people with ideas," said Pierce.

It sounded vaguely insulting, but Pierce had fixed Norman with the most charming smile he'd ever seen. "You and I are the kind who just get the job done."

Norman felt he was in the presence of a man of limitless understanding and wisdom.

"Norman, don't you think a company with twice as many staff departments as line departments is a little out of control?"

"What do you mean?" said Norman.

"I mean that only a third of this company is working on its business. Two thirds is just overhead."

Norman ran a staff department, and he disliked being classified as overhead. "Biotechnology is a complex business."

"So is paper manufacture," said Pierce. "But I have experience doing that with almost no staff effort."

Norman didn't understand what paper manufacture

had to do with anything, but he thought it better to say nothing while Pierce unburdened himself, which he seemed to need to do.

"This company is organized as a classic industrial hierarchy," said Pierce. "I will change that. I am going to tear down walls, and we're all going to reinvent the way we do business."

Norman nodded.

"We are going to make change here," said Pierce. "It will not happen easily."

Norman nodded.

"Have you ever seen a man go to the scaffold, Norman?"

"Do you mean like a construction worker?" Norman had the feeling he might be in the presence of a madman.

Pierce apparently thought Norman was being facetious, because he ignored the question. "I saw one go to the scaffold once," he said. "The man was an obstacle to change, and I believe he knew it. Nevertheless, I think he faced his destiny with great courage. And why not? There was no way on Earth he could change it, so why not accept it with grace, dignity, and courage?"

Norman wished the meeting was over. Company hysteria, paper manufacture, the scaffold — it was hard to keep one's balance listening to this man.

"Until we get through this difficult transition," said Pierce, "I'm going to be involved personally in every aspect of the company's affairs. On matters of any significance I want you to call me, any hour of the day or night. I'm still wrapping up another turnaround, so I'm not usually available during the day, but you can leave a detailed message on the voice mail. At night, you can usually get me directly. It doesn't matter what time it is. Do you understand?"

Norman wondered when Pierce ever slept.

"Do you have any questions about anything?"

Of course he did.

"No," said Norman.

Pierce stood up from the coffee table and started to walk back toward his desk, still holding his organization chart. "I'm glad we understand each other."

Norman stood up and wondered if he was supposed to follow him back to the other side of the room.

But Pierce dropped the paper on his blotter, turned around, folded his arms in front of him, and leaned up against the desk. He unfolded his arms and opened them in a gesture that was simultaneously dismissive and supplicating.

It was a courtly gesture, so much more civilized than Pressman's method of closing a meeting, which was to simply say, "Get back to work."

"If you'll excuse me," said Pierce, "I have to check the voice mail now."

Norman bent to pick up his budget report from the coffee table and started toward the door.

"Remember, Norman," said Pierce. "The people with the ideas."

Norman nodded and pulled the door open. He stepped through and pulled it closed behind him. Through the window in the reception area he could see a pinkness spreading across the sky. He looked at his watch. It was already ten minutes to seven.

Norman headed for the elevator. He wanted to get a snack in the company cafeteria to silence the grumbling of his empty stomach.

On the ground floor, he walked to the back of the building and joined a small group of secretaries and clerks who were waiting at the door of the cafeteria, which was to open at seven. Norman recognized two supervisors from the Strategic Planning Department, young men in white shirts with neckties and no jackets, who were chatting.

Norman tried not to listen, but couldn't avoid it.

"They say the hole in his head was as big around as your fist."

"No kidding?"

"Blood all over the inside of the car."

"Do you think he was *trying* to be messy about it?"

"I know I would. Me, I probably would have done it in Pressman's office, just to see if I could mess up his suit."

"Hell, I would have done it on his desk — no, in his lap."

"Do you think he would have sat still for it?"

They both laughed at that. Then one of them spoke more seriously to the other.

"Do you know if they'll get down as far as us?"

"What I heard was that *all* management staff at every level would get the axe and then about half would be invited back."

"Oh, God. Half. I wonder if I have any bullets at home."

The two of them laughed again.

"Maybe we'll get the notices tomorrow," said the serious one. "They like to do those things on Friday."

"What caliber do you think it was to make a hole like that?"

The door to the cafeteria opened to reveal its manager. He recognized Norman and nodded. Then he fastened the door against the fixture on the wall behind and stepped aside to let them enter. The dining area was redolent of coffee, bacon, and hash browns. Light poured in through the windows of the opposite wall as the sun rose over the parking lot outside. Utensils clattered behind the counter, somebody laughed near the cash register.

Norman tried to go in, but the cafeteria manager grabbed his jacket sleeve as he walked past. The man looked around to make sure everyone else was out of earshot.

"Have you heard anything, Norman?"

"All the vice presidents and directors got it," said Norman. "Last night or early this morning, I think."

"Oh, God." The man went pale. "I've got a mortgage. I've got a kid in college."

"I just met the new guy, and he said he's not going to do anybody else," said Norman.

"No?" The panic in the man's face turned to hope. He grabbed Norman's other jacket sleeve. "Let me get you some coffee and a bagel — on the house."

Norman let himself be led by the sleeve over to the counter. Managers were not ordinarily so demonstrative, and he was wary. But he stuck his budget report up under his arm and accepted the warm bagel on a paper plate, and coffee in a paper cup. The cafeteria manager got him a little package of cream cheese from the refrigerated case.

"Here, take this, Norman."

"Thanks," said Norman. "Do you have a doughnut?"

"You're sure they're not going to do anybody else?" whispered the man.

"He's even bringing back the people who got laid off," said Norman. "That's what he told me. Do you have a doughnut?"

"Really?" The cafeteria manager looked like a man who'd been told his terminal disease was a misdiagnosis.

"Except Blankenship." Norman looked at the floor. He didn't like people to forget about Blankenship.

"Yeah, I guess it's a little late for him," said the cafeteria manager. "Hey, enjoy your bagel. I'm going into my office to call my wife."

Norman looked down at his bagel. But when he looked up, the man was already halfway across the room on his way to his office. Norman decided the cafeteria manager was not one of the employees Pierce wanted to be told about. No ideas there. Norman went to find a seat by himself at an empty formica-topped table. It occurred to him that Pierce was right. The company was on the verge of hysteria. He chewed his bagel and mulled over his meeting with Pierce.

The venture group had obviously sent in a hatchet man, but he wasn't your ordinary hatchet man. He had fired a dozen vice presidents and directors, but he talked like he cared about the company's employees. Norman knew from long experience that your chances of surviving a new manager were better if you watched what he did than if you listened to what he said. This one seemed to know a great deal about market strategies, but he obviously knew very little about Human Resources. And Norman did not think it was a particularly effective approach to begin a meeting with a manager by telling him you're abolishing his department, even if Pierce was only kidding.

The bagel was dry in his mouth, and he took a sip of coffee to moisten it.

Norman's first order of business was to schedule a meeting of the Human Resources Department to tell his staff about the new turnaround specialist. He thought about the department. It consisted of three exempt staff, including himself, and two nonexempts. The two non-exempts, Cheryl and Louise, were admins. He wasn't sure what they did, since he left the supervision of them to the Assistant Manager, Jacqueline. Jacqueline was probably his biggest problem. She was extremely ambitious, and she was likely to make herself conspicuous in the misguided belief that the turnaround was an opportunity to increase her power and status.

Norman looked down at the paper plate in front of him. The bagel was gone, and he wondered what happened to it. He looked in his coffee cup, and it was empty. He looked at his watch and saw it was eight o'clock already. The cafeteria was filled with people, and the noise level had risen considerably. Norman shrugged, took the cup and plate to the trash can, and started toward his office.

When he arrived on the third floor, Cheryl and Louise were at their desks in the Human Resources Department reception area. Louise's elaborate hair was very large this morning. She was rummaging in her purse while Cheryl spoke to her, and Norman could tell the conversation was not amicable.

"It's called metonymy, Louise," said Cheryl, "and it's critical to understanding that book, and just about every other book you read, for that matter."

Louise took a can of hair spray from her purse, shook it, and then aimed a noisy contrail of lacquer vapor toward her hair. "I can't hear you," she said. "I'm spraying my hair."

"Good morning," said Norman. He could taste the hair spray in the air and he did not find it pleasant, but he tried to keep his expression neutral.

"Good morning, Norman." Louise clicked the cap back into place on her hair spray can.

"Hi." Cheryl looked dismissively at Norman, then resumed her harrying of Louise. "You should care about this, Louise," she said. "It's an important concept."

Louise uncapped the hair spray can and aimed another blast at herself.

Norman wondered if it wouldn't do her more good to aim the hair spray at Cheryl. From the day Cheryl had first arrived at Biomethods, Louise showed signs of insecurity and resentment, apparently because Cheryl had a master's degree in English literature when Louise had been no higher than junior college. To match Cheryl's educational attainments, Louise had developed larger and larger hair. Cheryl, in turn, countered Louise's hair by giving her lectures on concepts such as synecdoche and didacticism. This was especially upsetting to Louise, who considered herself an avid reader. Cheryl's lectures would drive her into a frenzy of hair-teasing and spraying, which Cheryl countered with more lectures, and so on in a vicious cycle Norman saw no hope of interrupting.

As he sought the protection of his office, Norman wondered if breathing hair spray wasn't damaging his lungs.

*   *   *

Norman called his meeting for that afternoon.

He prepared notes on the newsprint flip chart in the department conference room: NEW MANAGEMENT, NEW GOALS, NEW POLICIES, NEW STRUCTURE. He was waiting for his staff beside his flipchart when they arrived for the meeting.

When the four of them filed in, Louise and Cheryl took chairs as far from each other as possible, at opposite corners of the conference table. Jacqueline, as Assistant Manager, sat at the end opposite Norman, and Tim sat next to Louise, where he was hidden from Norman's view by her hair. But he was a benefits specialist and had never been particularly visible anyway.

They all stared at Norman's flipchart, and the only sound was the soft report of Louise's chewing gum, which crackled with the sound of someone crumpling sheets of old paperwork. Norman wondered if her hair was very heavy. He supposed that the exercise of the chewing somehow conditioned her neck muscles to help her keep her head upright.

Jacqueline, at the other end of the table, was wearing her power suit, the gray one with the chalk stripe, and Norman knew it could be a difficult meeting. He hated it when she wore her power suit.

He decided he should begin with an inclusion exercise.

"Before we begin," said Norman, "I think we should go around the room and each of us will describe something good that's happening in their personal life."

He wasn't looking at Jacqueline, but from the corner

of his eye he saw her stiffen. It didn't surprise him. Jacqueline disliked inclusion exercises.

He decided to start the exercise with Louise, hoping she might leave off chewing her gum while she told them about her good experience. "Louise, why don't you start."

"I read a good book," said Louise.

"What's it about?" said Norman.

"A vampire from New Orleans who's a rock star."

Norman wondered how a vampire could be a rock star. Weren't they supposed to be nobility or something?

"He's hundreds of years old," said Louise, "but looks young enough to be in rock music."

Cheryl coughed ostentatiously. Everybody turned to look at her.

"The book is egregiously self-referential." Cheryl seemed to address her remarks to everyone in the room but Louise. "The narrator spends pages and pages discussing the author's last book. I mean, does that break frame or what?"

"Have you read the book, too?" said Norman.

"Well, the reader needs to know where he came from." Louise seemed offended, and Norman worried the conversation might get out of hand.

"The original book was inspired," said Cheryl. "Telling the story from the vampire's point of view was innovative. But why did the author just do the same thing again? Isn't art about stretching aesthetic boundaries?"

"How would you know?" Louise's tone implied that Cheryl's hair was not big enough for artistic understanding.

Norman was worried that the meeting was slipping from his control. Cheryl started to answer Louise's challenge, but Jacqueline cut her off.

"I don't think we're here to discuss books or vampires," she said.

Everyone in the room turned toward her. She was as unlike either of her two subordinates as Norman could possibly imagine. She wore her black hair short and casual. She affected no makeup that he could discern. Her suit was fashionably severe. Her only concession to adornment was a pair of electric blue contact lenses that gave her an appearance simultaneously sinister and comical.

Jacqueline's job was to manage employee orientation and training programs, to supervise the support staff in Human Resources, and to manage nonexempt compensation. She was an outstanding performer and one of the best supervisors Norman had ever seen. And she was far too passionate about her job to be really happy in it.

Jacqueline wasn't smiling, but she swelled visibly as she became the center of attention. Norman wondered how she always seemed to take control of his meetings with a single remark.

"Norman has something to tell us," said Jacqueline.

Everyone looked at Norman.

"Maybe we'll just skip the books and move on to our discussion," he said.

Then he made some remarks about change and the need to work together in uncertain times. He was careful not to share with them anything about Pierce beyond his name. Any expectations they developed now could make Pierce's re-engineering campaign much more difficult. So he kept his remarks at the level of generalities. He saw their eyes glazing over as he talked about the need to understand company objectives and not just work for the department. He wondered why they weren't more interested in this stuff.

"Until we get some direction from the new management," he said, "it's business as usual." He looked around the room and saw they were all having a tough time keeping their eyes open. "You are to work on your existing objectives. I don't want anyone developing any new projects or trying to work up high-profile activities. The company is in the hands of a turnaround specialist. He will be happy with us if we just keep things moving steadily and quietly for the time being."

Then he woke them up and sent them back to their desks. But Jacqueline asked if she could stay and talk with him privately.

Norman shrugged and sat down. Jacqueline walked over to the door and closed it, then came back and sat in a chair near him.

Norman didn't know what she wanted, but he knew it would be difficult. She was not one to leave him in suspense. She got right to the point.

"Norman," she said, "I have an idea for a new product."

Even coming from Jacqueline it surprised him.

"Jacqueline," he said, "what are you talking about? You're a Human Resources manager, you're not concerned with products."

"But it's a fantastic concept," said Jacqueline.

"I'm sure it is," said Norman. "But we are the Human Resources Department. You should be working on Human Resources problems."

"We don't have any problems, Norman. This department's mission is to fill out forms."

"So?" said Norman. "Why aren't you figuring out better ways to fill out forms?"

"This is the nineties, Norman." Jacqueline aimed her eyes at him steadily. "Ideas can come from anywhere. Have you ever heard of re-engineering?"

Why did everybody want to browbeat him with re-engineering? "I've heard a little about it here and there."

"It's a way of re-evaluating everything an organization does," said Jacqueline.

"Jacqueline," he said, "we're in the hands of a turn-around specialist. We don't know what's going to happen. This is not the time to be talking about re-engineering." A part of Norman noted the reflexive idea-damping in his voice, and he regretted saying it as soon as it was out of his mouth. "Or a new product," he added lamely.

"Norman, I wouldn't be using up your time on this if it wasn't important."

Norman shifted himself in his chair, not knowing if he should feel flattered, manipulated, or both. "Why are you bringing this idea to me, anyway?"

"I tried to talk with those dolts in Marketing & Licensing about it, and they laughed at me. I think I should bring this idea to the new guy. I have to see him right away, before the Marketing morons wake up and see how good an idea it is. If I ask him for a meeting he'll put me off, but you've already met with him. If you ask for a meeting he'll see you right away."

Her reasoning seemed convoluted to Norman. But he knew her to have a much more sophisticated understanding of organizations than he did, and it occurred to him that maybe Jacqueline was one of the people Pierce was talking about. One of the people with ideas. "What is this product idea?"

Jacqueline stared at him as if she were weighing whether or not it was safe to tell him. Finally, she seemed to decide she could trust him. "We do genetic mapping here, right?"

"I think so," said Norman.

"My idea is that we map psychographic profiles to the human genome."

"I don't understand," said Norman.

Jacqueline looked at him as if she didn't really expect him to understand, and he wondered if he should be offended.

"I think we can find the human genes responsible for consumer buying behavior."

"Why would we even want to?" said Norman.

"To develop a simple blood test that would predict

what kinds of products and services people are likely to buy. It would be a new frontier in direct marketing."

A laugh began to work its way into the back of Norman's throat, but as soon as he was aware of it he suppressed it. Jacqueline was staring at him quite earnestly, and he did not want to show himself to share any attitudes with the dolts in Marketing & Licensing. They were a line department and liked to lord it over the staff departments. They knew nothing of the intricacies involved in supporting an organization of this size.

"How about it, Norman? Will you take me to see the new guy? He would want you to, you know."

"It's crazy." Norman tried to say it sympathetically.

"There was a time when flying was crazy," said Jacqueline.

Norman didn't know what to say. He hated to travel, and he thought flying *was* crazy. But Pierce did say he wanted Norman to help him find the people with ideas.

"All right," he said.

It was the first time that day Jacqueline smiled at him.

Two

NORMAN had a lot of work to do, and it was late in the day before he had the chance to call Pierce about Jacqueline's idea. It was dark outside when he picked up the phone and punched in Pierce's number. He got the voice mail, which told him, in Pierce's voice, that his boss was either away from his desk or on another line and to leave a message.

Norman looked at his watch. It was five-thirty. He hated being here past five, and the kids expected him home by six-fifteen with macaroni and cheese, since it was Thursday. He left a message that he needed to talk with Pierce and to please call him. Then he tapped in a pause command while he tried to decide how it would look if he asked Pierce to call him at home. He remembered Pierce's remarks about the scaffold, and he wondered whether it looked more courageous to open his home life to Pierce or to keep it closed off. Then he realized he was being ridiculous. What did the scaffold have to do with his kids getting their macaroni and cheese? He punched in the resume command and recited his home telephone number.

On the way home he stopped at the crowded take-out place with dozens of other managerial and professional suburbanites, and reduced the six point four billion chicken population by two along with two large orders of macaroni and cheese and fresh garden salad. The kids loved macaroni and cheese, even the drippy stuff at the take-out place. As long as they ate their salads first, he'd let them eat as much as he bought. He wished his kids could have the macaroni and cheese with the orange-and-brown crust on it like his mother used to make. But the only way they could have that was if he made it for them. He would have liked to, but who had time? Maybe this weekend.

He came in the house and said good-bye to the babysitter, who, as usual, was waiting at the door when he walked in. He left the packages of dinner on the counter in the kitchen and went into the family room. His eight-year-old son was kneeling on the carpet in front of the big-screen television, watching an infomercial in which a man was exhorting a room full of people to believe in themselves.

"Did you get macaroni and cheese?" The boy spoke without looking up from the television.

"Did you do your homework?" Norman touched the boy's shoulder and felt relaxation suffuse his hand and then travel up his arm. Touching his son always felt like plugging himself into a recharging device: it relaxed him and energized his humanity.

"Homework's for squids." The boy looked up at Norman and smiled to emphasize his observation.

"Until you're out of school, consider yourself a mollusk," said Norman.

"You mean like a clam?"

Norman was pleased his son had his phyla straight. Norman had studied biology in college, and he knew it was sometimes difficult to tell a primate from a mollusk. Since becoming a Human Resources manager, he had learned that a lot of people *are* squids.

"No," said Norman. "You're a lot more mobile than that." The man on the television had chosen someone from the studio audience and was challenging him to believe in himself. "You know," said Norman, "believing in yourself is nice, but it really doesn't matter how much you believe in yourself if you don't do your homework."

"This guy says if you believe in yourself and order his cassette tape, you can be a millionaire."

Norman tousled the boy's hair. "You don't want to be a millionaire. You have to hang around with Republicans." He almost added "like your mother," but he was afraid his son would think he was ridiculing her.

The boy laughed, and Norman realized he liked to have his father tousle his hair.

"Come on," said Norman, "it's time to get ready for dinner."

*   *   *

Norman was able to top off his charge when his ten-year-old daughter came downstairs and gave him a hug. He never tired of the routine. She called him "Daddy" and hugged him as if he'd been gone a week. He thought it was all the more wonderful because he knew it wouldn't last. It couldn't be but another three or four years before she started on the next stage of her life and became too self-conscious to hug him. He knew it would be another ten years after that before the two of them could get beyond the awkwardness of it to hug again.

Despite the recharging from his daughter, Norman was exhausted by the time he got the kids fed and put the dinner for Gwen and him in the microwave. He sent the kids to get ready for their baths and went to unload the dishwasher. He had a fistful of forks and spoons when Gwen came through the kitchen door.

Norman didn't drop his silverware or allow her to set her briefcase down before he grabbed her and kissed her deeply, seeking yet another charging for his dying battery. She responded warmly to the kiss. As soon as it was finished, she began talking about her day.

"It's finally happening," she said. "Rod asked me to honcho the Human Resources accounting project. He said to me, and these are his exact words, he said to me, 'I want real accounts set up. I want something we can manage.' "

Norman liked to see his wife happy. And he was glad

she was too excited to remember their argument from the night before. Maybe they would be able to bury it again.

"Gee, that's great. By the way, the kids are getting ready for their baths."

"I'll just say hello to them." She finally began unbuttoning her coat. "You finish making dinner." She hurried toward the doorway, shucking her coat as she walked, then stopped. She turned around, one arm still in a sleeve, and her eyes shone as brightly as they had the day their daughter was born.

"I'm supposed to give a presentation on it this weekend at the company-wide meeting. If I can make it work, it could mean a vice presidency."

"I know you can make it work." Norman had forgotten about her company-wide meeting. He had gotten Gwen to agree not to stay over Saturday night, but she was going to have to be there all day both days of the weekend.

She smiled broadly, then headed off toward the bathroom.

Norman wondered how Gwen would have liked working for Pierce. She had such a strong leadership quality that she probably would be in constant conflict with him. But she had so many ideas. Was she one of the ones he was so interested in?

Half an hour later, Gwen had extracted a promise from the kids to put on clean pajamas after their baths were finished, and she came into the dining room to sit down at the table Norman had laid.

"Anything new at work today?"

"The venture people sent us a turnaround specialist," said Norman. "The executive team is gone."

Gwen lit up at the prospect of new information, but before she could pump Norman for details the telephone rang out in the kitchen. They looked at each other.

"You got dinner." Gwen stood up. "It's my turn for the telephone."

Norman shrugged and sagged back against his chair.

He could hear her talking in the kitchen, although he couldn't make out anything specific. But she was gone for more than a minute, so he assumed it was her call. Probably someone from her staff making more arrangements for the weekend meeting.

He was chewing his third or fourth bite when Gwen returned to the dining room.

"It's for you."

He looked with both annoyance and puzzlement at the remaining chicken. "Is it Pierce?"

Gwen nodded as she sat down. "What a charming man."

It's funny she would describe him that way. Norman felt rather like that about him, too, and he and Gwen didn't often like the same people. He tossed his napkin on the table without folding it and stood up. "Don't wait for me."

Norman wondered if Gwen had pumped Pierce for information about his turnaround strategy. He wouldn't doubt it. Gwen was pretty good at getting information from people. It was one of the things that made her so effective in her job. If she had, however, he felt confident she had gotten nothing more than the chicken population and some execution anecdotes. Gwen was good, but he didn't think she was a match for Pierce. He picked up the phone.

"Norman. You called today." Pierce's soothing voice made him forget about his unfinished chicken. "What can I do for you?"

Norman told him about Jacqueline and that she had an idea for a product he would prefer she explained to him herself. He reminded his boss at several points in the explanation that Pierce had asked him to help find employees like Jacqueline.

Pierce questioned him a little, then made a decision.

"Bring her to my office tomorrow at six p.m. The three of us will talk about this together."

* * *

The next day, Jacqueline seemed pleased at the idea of meeting with Norman and Pierce, and it occurred to Norman that she felt it as important to get close to power as to have her ideas heard. In fact, it was probably even more important. Maybe she would grow out of that some day.

Norman spent the entire day on the paperwork associated with Blankenship's death. He had been putting it off since the day it happened, partly because of the strange feelings he had about the whole matter. But on this day he got down to work on it. He had to pull Blankenship's file and re-file it in the Inactive section. Then he had to fill out medical insurance forms for Blankenship's family so they could continue to use the plan for a while. He had to issue a Termination Memo to Payroll, and he had to cancel any training courses for which Blankenship had been registered. He had to issue an Employee Deletion Memo for Tim, who maintained the Employee Telephone Directory, and he had to issue cancellations for Blankenship's i.d. and radiation badges and his corporate American Express card. He had to write a memo to redeem his business-associated frequent flyer miles. It's amazing how much paperwork an employee suicide creates. He felt rather proud of the thoroughness with which he'd effaced the dead man's presence.

It being Friday, most of the staff had cleared out of the office before five. Norman sat at his desk doing nothing as the darkness crept over the parking lot outside. Blankenship's car had been in the nearest row of the far lot that day. Norman hadn't seen anything until Blankenship had actually shot himself, but his mind replayed for him its own version of the event regularly.

He saw Blankenship leaving his boss's office with a stony face. His boss might even have been a little concerned that Blankenship looked like he was taking the news of his layoff too calmly. The man didn't go back to his own desk, but after handing in his i.d. card walked out to his car. He climbed in the car, opened the glove compartment, and took out a pistol he kept there. It was a .38 probably, or maybe a nine millimeter. Norman imagined Blankenship then turning the gun upside down and putting the muzzle into his mouth. It clicked against his teeth, and its metallic taste was strange but not really unpleasant. He moved the muzzle around a little until he was sure it was pointing directly at the roof of his mouth, then he grabbed the cross on its chain around his neck with his left hand while he pulled the trigger with his right.

There was an explosion, but there was no real pain, just a hazy surprise that he was still alive. Then he regretted that the one bullet gave him time to reconsider his decision. When Norman got there, he was grateful to spend his last moments with another person. That was why he gave Norman the cross, out of gratitude.

Norman felt the cross through his shirt. He was glad he'd been there to give Blankenship some comfort in his final moments. He was satisfied — humbly satisfied, somehow — that his presence had been a support for another human being in a time of great stress.

"Norman?"

He looked up. Jacqueline was standing in the doorway, staring at him with eyes the color and intensity of the flames on a gas range. He glanced at his watch and saw it was a few minutes to six.

"Time to go, huh?" He got up and looked around his office. He decided he'd just leave his coat and briefcase here and stop back to get them after the meeting. "I imagine an evening meeting spoils your weekend, Jacqueline." He hoped Gwen got home early to be with the kids, as they'd agreed. The babysitter didn't like to have to stay late, and they couldn't afford to lose this one.

"You don't have to worry about that, Norman."

He looked at Jacqueline, and she looked as serious as ever. She was wearing another power suit. He wasn't sure, but he thought the stripe was even more pronounced this time. Norman supposed that was the essence of power dressing: some small bizarre flaw, like a bright yellow necktie or an excessive stripe, that allowed the wearer the illusion of having personal taste in clothing.

Norman wondered if Pierce would be equal to dealing with Jacqueline or if anything would come of her product idea.

"Shall we go then?"

Jacqueline stepped out of the doorway to let him pass and lead the way to Pierce's office on the fifth floor.

They walked in silence to the elevator. Norman knew he should probably make small talk with her, but to be perfectly honest he didn't particularly like Jacqueline, and he didn't like talking with her very much. She apparently felt the same about him. So they rode without speaking.

The fifth floor was as deserted as the Human Resources Department on the third floor, and most of the lights were off. Norman and Jacqueline walked through the gloom to Pierce's office.

They stepped around the secretary's empty desk, and Norman tapped on the door. It was thirty-six hours since he had last done this.

"Come in," said Pierce's voice, and the door opened into the same inky shadows Norman had seen in here before. Jacqueline seemed taken aback a little, but Norman walked into the darkness toward the halogen desk lamp as naturally as if he'd taken a B-school course on meeting your boss in the dark.

Pierce was standing in the shadows behind the desk.

"Pierce," said Norman, "this is Jacqueline. She's the Assistant Manager of Human Resources."

"Please sit down," said Pierce.

There were two chairs facing his desk, so Norman sat in one. He noticed as he sat that the desk lamp was arranged to shine directly into his eyes. He looked away and saw Jacqueline fumbling a little to seat herself in the other chair. She was not unattractive in this light. From the side, Norman couldn't see her contact lenses. Her black hair gleamed where the light caught it, and when she turned her head to look away from the desk lamp she showed an expanse of creamy white neck.

Norman thought he discerned movement on the other side of the desk, and he wondered if Pierce might shake hands this time. But the movement stopped.

"I'm glad to meet you, Mr. Pierce," said Jacqueline.

"Please, Jacqueline," said the dark shape behind the desk lamp, "just call me Pierce. Norman tells me you have a product idea."

"That's right," said Jacqueline.

"There's a reorganization under way." Pierce did not step into the light, and he looked as featureless as a shadow — a short one — behind the desk.

"And a new leadership more open to new ideas, I hope," said Jacqueline.

Norman, first squinting into the desk lamp, then looking back at Jacqueline, felt more like he was watching television than participating in a business meeting. He wondered if he should try to contribute anything.

"It's not very common for product development plans to come out of Human Resources," said the shadow.

Norman was surprised that Pierce appeared to be trying to discourage her. This seemed a reversal of his earlier strategy of tearing down walls.

"No company can prosper if it evaluates ideas by their source rather than their merit," said Jacqueline. "In the nineties new ideas can come from anywhere. Don't you believe in re-engineering?"

Norman expected Pierce to whip out his blank paper, but his boss just sounded cagey.

"Fads and fashion," said the shadow.

Then Norman realized that Pierce was goading Jacqueline. This was some sort of strategic maneuver.

"Not at all," said Jacqueline. "It's an idea whose time has come. At least for this company."

Nobody spoke for what seemed a minute or more. Norman looked at Jacqueline, who shaded her eyes as she stared defiantly toward the desk lamp. She knew just how risky this behavior was, but it would probably pay off for her. Norman realized that he didn't understand people who take risks, and then he remembered Pierce's remarks about acts of courage. He looked back toward the desk lamp and the dark shape behind it, but he couldn't see anything back there now.

Then things happened too quickly for him to comprehend. He thought he heard a rustling off toward his side, but before he could look, something passed in front of the halogen desk lamp, and he realized it was Pierce's head. The man's face, completely enshrouded in darkness, was suddenly directly in front of his own, about six inches from it, blocking out the desk lamp and filling his field of vision, such as it was.

"I must tell you," said Pierce in a soft, relaxed monotone, "how gratifying it is to see such self-assertion in the junior management staff. Where have you been hiding this young woman, Norman?"

Norman smelled the soapy odor of his breath again. He started to say something, but his tongue and lips were too dry. A kind of grunt issued from his throat.

"Oh, I wasn't asking for an answer, Norman." Pierce spoke in the soft tones of a veterinarian calming a nervous animal. "I just meant this is an unexpected level of management talent. This turnaround may proceed more easily than I expected."

Norman wanted to respond, but he didn't feel it was polite to cough or clear his throat when Pierce's face was so close to his.

"You're excused, Norman," said Pierce. "Jacqueline and I are going to talk about her product idea in more depth."

Norman was incredulous. He started to speak, but nothing came out. Then he finally cleared his throat. "You want me to leave?"

"Yes," said Pierce. "I think Jacqueline should have the opportunity to present her ideas without the intimidation of her supervisor's presence."

Norman almost laughed at that. Jacqueline had never shown any sign of being intimidated by him or anyone else at Biomethods.

"Won't you need my input?"

"I don't think so," said Pierce. He let a moment pass. "Please don't feel you're being excluded. I'll fill you in later."

Then, without making a sound, Pierce moved off toward Jacqueline's chair.

Norman felt there was nothing he could do but stand up and feel his way through the darkness to the doorway. When he safely got hold of the door handle, he turned to look at Jacqueline's chair. She was staring at Pierce, who had approached her just as closely as he had approached Norman. Pierce's white hair gleamed in the light of the desk lamp.

Pierce bent low over her, then moved around so his back hid her from Norman's view. He appeared to be whispering to her.

Instinctively, Norman shifted his gaze downward. He didn't know why Pierce might think it necessary to whisper to Jacqueline, but a tiny voice told him he should be embarrassed to watch. He turned back, opened the door, and stepped through as quickly as he could.

As he pulled the door closed behind him, he thought he heard a soft moan. It was not a sound of pain, but more like a deep and heartfelt sigh. At first he thought it might have come from Pierce, because it was not a sound he ever would have expected to hear from Jacqueline. But it was a sound from a feminine throat, not one he could imagine Pierce making.

He thought about going back into the office and demanding to know what was going on, but he felt like he didn't belong there. He walked toward the elevator with a strange feeling that he could only liken to embarrassment.

Three

NORMAN woke up alone on Saturday morning. Gwen had already left for her weekend meeting. He put on some jeans and a sweatshirt and went out to the living room. His son was watching an infomercial on television, in which ordinary people were being relieved of profound fatigue by eating an All-Natural Herbal Food Product.

"Where's your sister?" said Norman.

"Upstairs."

Norman watched the man on television make outlandish claims for the food product. "Justin, why are you watching this?"

"It's cool, Dad. This man here says he got rich from taking these pills."

Norman sat down beside him. "You can't get rich from taking pills."

"This guy did," said Justin.

Norman watched for a moment. The man actually insisted that he had suffered from severe fatigue until he began taking this product, whereupon he went from being poor and tired to being rich and energetic.

Norman stood up. "The guy's a squid. Can't you find some cartoons to watch?"

"I don't like cartoons," said the boy. "There's real estate on channel six, a food processor on channel thirteen, spray-on hair on channel—"

"Spray-on hair?"

"Yeah, it's really cool." Justin aimed the remote control at the television, and the energetic rich guy was replaced by a well-spoken and well-groomed woman who was spraying hair from an aerosol can on to the heads of a line of men suffering from male pattern baldness.

The woman explained how important hair was to both social acceptance and professional advancement.

Norman wished Justin liked cartoons, but he didn't think it would be possible to make him. "I'm going to get a shower," he said. "Then I'll fix you some breakfast."

* * *

After breakfast, Norman tried to call Jacqueline at home. He had some pretext in mind that he would ask if she knew how Tim was doing with the bonuses for the Marketing & Licensing Department, but he really just hoped she might tell him what happened in Pierce's office after he left.

"I can't come to the telephone right now," said Jacqueline. "Please leave your message after the beep."

Norman didn't leave a message. What was he going to say?

He remembered the moan he'd heard in Pierce's office. For all he knew Jacqueline might be spending the weekend with Pierce. He piled the kids into the car and went off to do the food shopping. They stopped at the town library and, while Justin and Megan looked over the shelves of recently arrived videos, Norman went to the desk to ask for the book about the vampire from New Orleans.

"Vampire?" said the librarian, a man about Norman's age with an apparently permanent expression of resentment. He furrowed his brow, which resettled his glasses on his nose. "New Orleans?" He tapped something into his computer terminal, managing to invest the action with considerable disgust. "Rock star?" He tapped something else into his terminal, then shook his head.

"No hits that intersect vampires, New Orleans, and rock stars. Here." He scribbled some numbers on a square of recycled paper. "This is the range of call numbers for the occult section. Maybe you can find it there."

The occult section was crowded. Norman had to sidle in among and peer around people to read the book titles, which covered astrology, witchcraft, parapsychology, alchemy, magic, angels, and pyramids. None of the books in the occult section seemed to be novels. He took one on near-death experiences and looked it over to see if it might offer some insight about the Blankenship event. It was written by someone who'd had a near-death experience (NDE, it was called) and had told it to someone else for organizing into book form. Norman read the first two pages. It read like something out of *Time* magazine. Norman had not trusted *Time* magazine ever since he'd learned it had darkened the photo of O. J. Simpson on its cover, presumably to make him look more menacing. Norman didn't think that darkening people made them look particularly menacing, but he was no less suspicious of *Time* magazine — or anybody who tried to write like it. He put the book back.

He wandered over to the management section, an area of the library he knew pretty well and usually had to himself. There were books on the corporate life cycle, organization development, leadership, and industrial psychology. His eye was drawn to the spine of a book with the word "turnaround" on it. He pulled it from the shelf. It was called *Anatomy of a Turnaround*. He turned it over and there was a picture of the author on the back. Late thirties, early forties. Short dark hair with a little bit of curl, glasses. His smile made Norman wonder if it weren't a humor book. But it appeared not to be. The author was a former bankruptcy lawyer and had seen dozens of turnarounds up close, according to the jacket flap. Norman looked at the picture again. The man's expression was too open and candid for a lawyer; maybe that was why he was a former one.

The book looked interesting, so he took it to the

counter and checked it out. Then he gathered up Justin and Megan, who said they couldn't find any videotapes they wanted to borrow. As Norman shepherded the kids out to the car, Justin pointed out that the library's video collection ran heavily to ballets, operas, and documentaries — material, he explained, that was favored by squids.

Saturday in the supermarket, with its oppressive crowds and myriad distractions, is not a place where one thinks about anything other than surviving the process of collecting food choices and conducting them safely through a check-out line. The kids didn't particularly want to be there, and Norman had to watch them every moment to make sure they didn't wander away to be kidnapped or do something to embarrass him.

Norman found himself at one point in a brief conversation with his son over a refrigerated display of upmarket cheese.

"Here's one." Justin offered him a chunk of white American cheese in plastic wrap.

"That's not what I need." Norman laid aside a wrapped wedge of sharp cheddar that was a little too large and took a smaller one from under it.

"It's cheese," said Justin.

"You couldn't prove it by me." Norman moved along the cold box and began to pick through the provolone.

"The label says it's American," said Justin.

"I have doubts about its loyalty," said Norman.

Justin laughed, and it lifted the fatigue from Norman's shoulders. Justin didn't expect him to have any ideas or be marked for leadership. He accepted him pretty much for what he was, and he laughed at his jokes.

The crowds and the traffic were so bad that it took nearly the rest of the day to get the shopping done. It was late in the afternoon when they got back to the house. He sent the kids off to amuse themselves while he tried to call Jacqueline's apartment. He got her machine again, so he gave up and started making macaroni and cheese for dinner. Most people think you just throw a lot of cooked macaroni into a dish with some processed cheese food, but that wasn't the kind of macaroni and cheese Norman wanted for his kids that weekend.

He put a layer of macaroni into the dish, then a layer of freshly grated cheddar cheese. Then he put in another layer of macaroni, followed by a layer of freshly grated provolone cheese. Then he put several dots of butter into the dish. There was plenty of time, so he sat down at the kitchen table with his library book before starting the next layer of macaroni. He stared at the wall of the kitchen and wondered if he wasn't poisoning the kids with all this cheese and butter. It hardly mattered. He couldn't help himself. They loved this stuff. It felt so good to give it to them.

He shrugged and opened the book. *Anatomy of a Turnaround* was a study of business turnarounds: why they happen, how they proceed, the effect they have on people. Norman learned that the turnaround specialist is the most powerful person in the business world.

> The turnaround expert works in an organization without belonging to it. He (for they are almost universally male) answers to no one within the organization. He may report to a trustee, a venture capital group, or another corporation, but he is an outsider and has no loyalties, no attachments, no relationships to incumbent employees. He shares none of their history, but more important than that, he knows he will not share their future, either.

The description made Pierce sound rather dangerous, and Norman found himself wondering again what was going to happen to the company and its employees. For that matter, he wondered what had happened to Jacqueline in Pierce's office. Was there a connection between this personality type (which obviously fit Pierce) and what Norman had witnessed?

Because the turnaround expert leaves when the restructuring is complete, he almost never sees the results of his work. His position is, in effect, one with great power and no responsibility. It takes a rare kind of person to enjoy this sort of work: one capable of nearly complete detachment, one motivated more by power than achievement, prestige, or gain. In fact, the turnaround specialist can be said to be motivated *exclusively* by power.

Norman didn't think he'd ever met anyone who was motivated exclusively by power. Even Jacqueline, who was more preoccupied with power issues than anybody he'd ever met, had occasional episodes, like her product idea, in which she showed some interest in achievement. What kind of person is motivated only by power? What kind of person wants to join a community (which is, after all, what a company is) and not belong to it? Maybe it was a person who made sketches, sat on coffee tables, waved around blank pieces of paper, and talked about executions. Maybe it was the kind of person that Norman, for all his training in psychology and organization development, could never understand.

Norman wondered, then, if he was taking the easy way out by telling himself he couldn't understand Pierce. Then he had to admit to himself that he was nursing a bit of resentment. He'd been told to leave the office while his new boss had a private meeting with his subordinate. He felt excluded and powerless. Was this what it was like to feel a hunger for power? Norman shook his head. No, he didn't feel hungry for power. He felt hungry for not being excluded. He felt hungry for affiliation.

He stood up from the table and walked over to the counter to start another layer of macaroni in the casserole dish. He repeated the cheese grating, the macaroni, the dots of butter. When he finally had all the layers in place, he poured a little bit of milk into the dish and topped it with bread crumbs. As he slid the dish into the oven, he noticed it was dark out.

He did not try to call Jacqueline's house again. He was afraid if he reached her, his resentment might sound in his voice. The last thing a manager wants with an employee like Jacqueline is to let her know he resents her.

He sat down with the kids in the dining room shortly after he took the casserole out of the oven. It was late and Gwen wasn't home yet, but the kids hardly seemed to notice her absence. Norman ate macaroni and cheese, traded squid jokes with his son, and listened intently to his daughter's description of various acquaintances' transgressions of social protocol at school. It occurred to him, as she described how alliances and relationships shifted in response to things like too much enthusiasm in conversation or wearing white socks on Tuesday, that the social order at her school was at least as calculated as that of fourteenth-century Florence. He wondered if her school weren't in need of re-engineering. He imagined himself reorganizing the place, waving a blank piece of paper, suspending students, and laying off teachers.

Gwen came in the door after they'd finished the casserole and the salad. She had already had dinner with her staff, but she sat down to ice cream with Norman and the kids. She seemed energized from her off-site meeting. She took her turn joking and laughing with the kids, and as the four of them sat at the table eating ice cream Norman had that funny feeling that he often had with his kids, wishing for their bedtime at the same time he hoped the moment would last forever.

Finally, it was time to send them to their rooms, and he and Gwen were alone at the dining room table.

"Good meeting, huh?" said Norman.

Gwen sipped from her coffee cup. "It was fantastic, Norman. Fantastic." She took another sip. "Fantastic."

"The kids were good at the supermarket today."

"Norman, what happened at your meeting last night?"

Norman had stopped for a drink after the meeting, and got home too late to talk with Gwen about it.

"Nothing."

"Did Jacqueline present her idea to Pierce?"

"Yeah."

"And?"

Norman shrugged. "I don't know. I guess he's going to think about it."

Gwen looked a little impatient with him again. "He shouldn't let you be put in the middle like that."

Norman was surprised he felt that way himself. He shrugged. "I don't care very much."

Gwen smiled, and Norman thought there was a little sadness in it. "I'm sorry, dear," she said.

Norman didn't want sympathy just then. "Want to get ready for bed?"

They went into Justin's bedroom, and Gwen tucked him in while Norman watched. Then they did the same for Megan, doing her second because she was older and got to stay up a few minutes later.

Norman switched off the light, and as he and Gwen stepped into the hall she grabbed Norman's hand. She smiled at him as they walked down the hallway. Gwen was a woman of passions. She was passionate about her marriage, passionate about her kids, passionate about her job. It occurred to Norman that power was a motivator for Gwen. Maybe not a primary one, but a motivator nevertheless. It occurred to him he was surrounded by people hungry for power and that he'd never understood that before.

Gwen turned to him as they went into the bedroom and motioned for him to shut the door.

Norman closed the door and walked over and wrapped his arms around her. They kissed and rubbed themselves against each other, then slowly broke away. They each started to undress. Norman went into the bathroom, closed the door, and slipped his shirt off. He took the cross on its chain from around his neck and stuck it in his pants pocket, put his shirt back on, tucked it in, flushed the toilet, and went back into the bedroom.

Gwen kicked off her shoes, then she came up close to him again and began unbuttoning his shirt.

"How did your presentation go?" he said.

She smiled broadly. "Norman, it was fantastic. Standing O."

Norman wondered what it was like to give a speech for which everyone in your company gets to their feet to applaud. It must be such events that make people want to be leaders.

"They loved it." Gwen threw off her blazer and unbuttoned her blouse. "I talked with Rod afterward, and he asked me to have lunch with him in the Sky Room next week."

Rod was the CEO at Gwen's company, and the Sky Room was the company's VIP dining room. Norman knew something big was in store for her.

She threw her blouse on the bed and unbuttoned her skirt where it fastened at the hip, then stepped out of it before throwing it on the bed along with the blouse. She stood before him in black bra and pantyhose, which she began to roll down from her waist.

Norman grabbed her and felt her flesh and the roll of pantyhose around her hips against him. "Do you want to take a shower with me?"

Norman didn't think she particularly needed washing, but in the special code they had developed over twelve years of marriage an invitation to a shower implied an entire ritual. They would shower together, soaping each other gently and then taking turns under the shower head to rinse off. Then they would dry off and climb in between the sheets and make love. It was their way of marking major achievements, and it was part of the ceremony that the achiever was the one invited.

The shower went as he had imagined, and almost as soon as he climbed into bed her firm, satiny body was all over him. Desire surged through his groin. He stroked her breast, kissed her neck, nibbled her shoulder, and they moved quickly into energetic sex without making a sound. Gwen had always worried about the children hearing, and the two of them had the habit of utterly silent lovemaking. As always, he lost himself in the experience of her, and he was barely aware of her arching her back under him as he exploded in climax. He kissed her neck just behind her ear and then rolled off her. He reached over and stroked her shoulder before becoming comatose.

Norman woke up in the dark to an utterly silent house. He didn't know what had awakened him, but he realized he needed to use the bathroom. He pushed himself out of bed and padded into the master bathroom. His back felt raw. He closed the door and turned on the light, then had to stand without moving for what seemed like a half hour until his eyes could tolerate the light. He finally opened them and looked at his naked body in the mirror. He turned and looked over his shoulder at himself. There were about a dozen scratches in a herringbone pattern up his back. Three had broken the skin.

Gwen had scratched him during their lovemaking. He studied the welts over his shoulder and touched them. They were sore.

Why had she scratched him like that? Was she trying to make him hump faster or something? It occurred to him that the scratches were symbolic of their relationship. He loved her, but sometimes he wished she didn't have to always encourage him to hump faster.

After he'd finished in the bathroom and returned to bed, Norman rolled on to his side facing away from her and thought about his scratches. Sexual activity apparently had anesthetic properties. If he hadn't been orgasmic when Gwen scratched him, he'd probably have noticed she was doing it. He tried to imagine Gwen scratching him under other circumstances — watching television, say, or during a conversation. But he could not imagine himself sitting still for it. In the midst of sexual climax, he supposed, he could tolerate just about anything. He wondered if everybody was like that, or if it was just him. But he didn't think about it much before he fell asleep again.

*　　*　　*

Norman often got to work late the first day of the week. He never worried about arriving late, because Jacqueline habitually got there early and she was perfectly capable of running the office.

He strolled in at nine-thirty. Cheryl and Louise were both at their desks, which were piled with stacks of group insurance change requests. Biomethods, Inc. had four group insurance plans, counting the free policy for accidental death and dismemberment, and none of the company's employees seemed able to live a week without requesting a change from one to the other or making some sort of update. Much of the work of the Human Resources Department consisted of evaluating these requests for change and sorting them into piles of similar requests. That, apparently, is what Cheryl and Louise were doing when Norman walked in. They were both good at this work and could easily conduct a conversation while doing it.

"You could hardly have a better metaphor for the psychopath," said Cheryl. "The vampire lives among us but is not one of us."

"Yeah, they look at people and they just see food," said Louise.

"Louise," said Cheryl, "you don't *believe* in them, do you?"

"Hi, Norman," said Louise.

"Good morning," said Norman. He looked from Louise to Cheryl and smiled, so the greeting would cover her as well. He noticed Louise's hair spray can was not on her desk. It seemed the two admins had patched up their differences, whether permanently or temporarily Norman couldn't tell. He stood between their desks smiling stupidly and hoping they might resume their conversation and one of them would say the title of the book about the vampire rock star in New Orleans. He was determined not to ask for it.

But they just sat in silence and waited for him to leave. So he turned and walked toward Jacqueline's office. Before he reached the door, Cheryl called to him.

"She's not here, Norman."

Norman shrugged and went to his own office. It wasn't like Jacqueline to be late for work. When he entered his office he left the door open, and he could hear Louise and Cheryl resume their conversation.

"Well?" said Cheryl. "*Do* you believe in them?"

"There are more things in this world," said Louise, "than you can learn about in college."

Norman had to admit to himself that he was a little relieved Jacqueline hadn't come in yet. He was nervous about seeing her. He knew Jacqueline, and he knew that a private meeting with Pierce would somehow increase the power of her position in his department. There it was again. Power. This was getting tiresome. Norman shook off his depressing line of thought and prepared himself to start work.

Norman's current project was writing a managers handbook on employment law. The managers at Bio-methods were largely well-meaning people, but everybody has some sort of prejudice, and without guidance even a well-meaning person could blunder into age, sex, sexual orientation, race, or disabilities discrimination. Part of Norman's job was protecting the company from the lawsuits that could result from normal managerial behavior.

He had written something over thirty pages of the handbook so far, working from an outline he'd developed a month ago. He sat down at his desk and started up the computer. After it had loaded everything and was ready, he called up the handbook file. He saw that the next section was supposed to describe the Consolidated Omnibus Budget Reconciliation Act (COBRA). As he looked around the shelves in his office for his COBRA manual, the conversation out in the reception area drifted into his hearing.

"Think about it, Louise," said Cheryl. "If each one of them bites just one person a day and turns that person into one, and then that one bites one person a day, there would be a vampire population explosion."

"You don't always turn into one when you're bitten," said Louise. "Only if you're lucky."

Norman found the COBRA manual and began paging through it, wondering where to start. Basically COBRA is intended to set the parameters by which a company allows departing employees to continue in an organization's group insurance plan. These parameters filled many pages of the COBRA manual, and Norman thought it might be confusing to the Biomethods managers, who were mostly scientists and had a great deal of difficulty understanding anything that wasn't a gene location or knockout. So he decided the COBRA section of his handbook should consist of two sentences:

> Make no promises regarding the group insurance
> plan to departing employees. Always send them
> to the Human Resources office for debriefing.

"They don't usually kill you with a single bite," said Louise. "They want to keep you alive so they can bite you again and again."

"Like milking a cow?" said Cheryl.

"Sort of like that," said Louise.

"Why don't they save themselves a lot of trouble and just domesticate us?"

"How do you know they haven't?" said Louise.

Norman thought about turnaround specialists and the desire for power over others. Louise was right. There *are* more things in this world than you can learn about in college. He realized he was having trouble keeping his mind on his work, so he got up and closed his office door. He hoped it didn't look like he was shutting the door against Cheryl and Louise, although that was exactly what he was doing. He sat down again and tried to lose himself in the Drug-Free Workplace Act and the Employee Polygraph Protection Act.

He didn't know how long he'd been writing when he was conscious of a knock at the door.

"Yes?"

The door opened, and Pierce was standing in the doorway.

"Norman," he said, "I've just been to the Controller's Office. I asked them to cut a bonus check for Ackerman in Marketing & Licensing, and they said it required a transmittal form from you. Rather than make a fuss about it, I thought I would just come and ask you for the form."

Norman wanted to ask him where Jacqueline was, but something inside told him the question was inappropriate or presumptuous, or both.

"It takes three weeks to issue a bonus check," said Norman.

Pierce didn't say anything, so Norman elaborated.

"I need a Bonus Request Memo from the employee's manager. I log the request and forward it to the CFO for approval. When it comes back, I attach the Certification of Bonus Approval and I give it to Louise. She then sends Payroll a Request for Compensation and Withholding

Analysis. Payroll examines the employee's Year-to-Date Compensation and sends the employee's manager a Notification of Special Withholding, so the manager will know how much of the bonus will be withheld for payroll taxes. If we don't withhold from the check, the employee might have an unexpected tax bill at the end of the year. Sometimes the managers like to change the bonus recommendation then, so the employee will receive a larger check, net of withholding. If that's the case, the process begins again. Otherwise, the manager signs the Notification of Special Withholding and sends it to me. I add it to the Bonus File and send Accounting a Special Compensation Release."

"Then the check is issued?" said Pierce.

"The Release, as I understand it, goes into a Payables Account. It usually takes the Controller's Office a week after that to cut the check." Norman was irritated that Pierce seemed unimpressed by his mastery of this process. The creation of it represented a good deal of time and effort.

Pierce stepped into the office and closed the door behind him. He did not sit down but walked right up and stood in front of Norman's desk. Norman felt a little intimidated looking up, but he knew he was not expected to stand.

"This is unacceptable, Norman," said Pierce.

Norman wondered what he meant by "unacceptable." One might as well say gravity was unacceptable.

"When an employee does something worth a bonus," said Pierce, "the bonus must be issued immediately. I don't care about Certifications of Bonus Approval or Notices of Special Withholding."

"A bonus can't be paid without a Certification of Bonus Approval." Norman didn't want to be rude, but it was clear his boss was out of touch with reality.

Pierce didn't say anything. He took a pen from his breast pocket with one hand and with the other took the pad of yellow sticky notes from the holder on Norman's desk. He wrote a number on the top sticky note and peeled it from the pad. Then he reached across Norman's desk and pressed the sticky note against Norman's necktie. His fingertips felt like steel. Blankenship's cross, which was under Norman's shirt and happened to be between Pierce's fingers and Norman's chest, pressed into the skin.

"This is the amount of Ackerman's bonus," said Pierce. "Have a check prepared and deliver it to my office before you leave today. And it had better be before Ackerman leaves, too."

He turned, opened the door, and left without saying anything else.

Through a haze of embarrassment and humiliation, Norman saw that the office beyond was empty and quiet. Cheryl and Louise had apparently left for lunch already. He was glad nobody was around to see the yellow sticky note on his tie. He peeled it off and looked at it. He wondered what Ackerman had done to deserve this. He winced with embarrassment at the memory of Pierce sticking it on him.

Norman often thought the manager-subordinate relationship was similar to that of a doctor and a patient. He had only met Pierce a few days before, but he felt the man knew his weaknesses as intimately as if he had just read his medical file. He hoped he would treat the knowledge with as much privacy as he expected from a doctor, or a torturer.

He called Accounting and asked for an appointment with the Controller after lunch. The Controller's secretary, whom Norman had never found to be particularly cooperative, tried to put him off.

"This is at Pierce's request," said Norman.

"Will two-thirty be OK?" she said.

"That will be fine," said Norman.

Pierce's name could open doors around the company. Nobody knew what he might do or what he was capable of.

Norman hung up the telephone and walked into the outer office toward Cheryl and Louise's desks. The office was quiet. The few large stacks of forms on each desk were now many smaller, neater stacks. Norman walked over to Louise's desk and looked over the stacks. He didn't want to touch them because he suspected Louise had them exactly the way she wanted them.

When he looked up, Jacqueline was standing in front of him. She had approached so quietly that he was almost startled. Her skin was paler than he remembered, and her eyes were rimmed with red. The blue contact lenses created a rather unattractive but distinctly patriotic effect.

"Are you all right?" said Norman.

"Fine. I'm sorry I'm late." Jacqueline shifted her leather portfolio from her right to her left hand, then rubbed a small bruise on her neck with the right. Her movements were lethargic in a way that seemed unlike her and her voice was uncharacteristically soft and monotonous. "I overslept this morning."

"You don't look well, Jacqueline." Norman had never seen her look so tired. "Maybe you should go home and rest."

"I'm fine, Norman. I worked all weekend and I'm a little tired. That's all."

"What did you work on?"

"My product idea. Pierce wants me to work up a business plan."

"Well," said Norman, "there's not much going on here today. If you've finished the plan, you can go home."

"I'm certainly not finished." Jacqueline walked toward her office. "It takes a lot longer than one weekend to create a business plan."

"It does?" Norman had never worked on a business plan.

"Besides," she said over her shoulder, "I have a meeting with Pierce this evening."

As Norman watched her go into her office and close the door behind her, Cheryl and Louise returned, still deep in conversation.

"Think how many of them there would be if they all lived forever," said Cheryl.

"They don't live forever," said Louise, "just a very long time."

FOUR

PIERCE came to Vidalon-le-Haut in 1783. He arrived at the ravine near dawn on a clear morning in early fall. It was cold down in the valley next to the river, but Pierce never minded cold. As he approached the gate of the mill to present himself, an old man in a Phrygian cap stood slowly from a stool and wrapped his coat more tightly around him with one hand as he raised a lantern toward Pierce's face with the other. The cuffs of the old man's coat were frayed, and Pierce could see an ancient stain at the bottom of one of the patch pockets at his hip. A herald's bell fixed with a wooden handle rested on the ground by the stool, and Pierce hoped the old man was not going to shatter the quiet to announce him.

"I am Perce," he said, "here at the pleasure of Monsieur Montgolfier."

"Yes." The man squinted at his face by the lantern light, then looked him up and down. "You are expected. Follow this path, and take the left fork to the rear entrance of the house. Don't you need a light?"

"Thank you, no."

The sky was beginning to turn pink above the ravine, but in the shadow of the bluff the darkness was thick in the way Pierce preferred. He could see quite well without light, and he followed the old man's gesture toward the eclectic structure that housed the mill, its workers, and the Montgolfier family. An ancient farmhouse, it had apparently grown gables and annexes as they were needed over the years to house the hundred-odd families and the machinery they used to make fine paper from linen rags.

Pierce started up the path. The pebbles were sparse underfoot, and he thought the path overdue for new gravel. The mill was apparently not as prosperous as it could be. As the path approached the edge of a wide, gravel-paved roundabout for carriages, it forked. He took the fork that turned toward the back of the house, away from the round-about and the unlit main entrance of the house, a portal of declining grandeur. The path took him toward a servants' entrance with a dim light in the window next to the door. This was appropriate, he supposed, for a candidate for the position of secretary.

At this smaller door, Pierce presented his credentials to a servant who was much younger and better dressed than the old man at the gate. He wore knee breeches and a dark coat but no wig. His hair was fastened at the back of his head with a dark ribbon. His appearance was healthy and vital, but Pierce had fed two days ago on the road and paid him little attention.

The young man took the letter of introduction and told Pierce to wait by the light of a single candle on a rough bench in a sparsely furnished room obviously intended for tradesmen.

Having traveled across a continent and a sea to get to Vidalon-le-Haut, Pierce was pleased with the opportunity to sit quietly and reflect on why he had come. It was not that he required rest. Pierce rarely needed rest. But one did require the occasional opportunity for reflection.

Pierce had come to Vidalon-le-Haut because of an air-borne sheep.

Several months previous, the Montgolfier brothers, Joseph and Etienne, had constructed a vessel for sailing the air. They had made an enormous bag of linen and pa-per and filled it with buoyant gases, then used it to send aloft a duck, a rooster, and a sheep. They called it a *ballon dirigeable*.

One such as Pierce, whose only natural enemy was

ennui, could not ignore such an event. He imagined himself voyaging above the clouds. There must be immense power in seeing the world from that perspective, flying untethered across the vault of heaven. He had discovered they were paper manufacturers and that their epochal ideas extended beyond airborne sheep. They were among the principal proponents of a new social order as well.

The Montgolfier mill provided clean, safe, orderly conditions for its workers, in both work and residence. The Montgolfiers were generous with festivities and payment, and the mill provided work on a fixed schedule for those willing to submit to its discipline. That work could be disciplined and organized for the purpose of supporting an enterprise was a strange notion in 1783, and Pierce knew it had probably met opposition here in this provincial river valley.

The servant returned and told Pierce the Messieurs Montgolfier were ready to receive him. He led him by lamplight along a darkened hallway bounded on either side by idle millworks. They passed room after room of unattended pulping vats and empty drying racks until they reached what appeared to be workers' quarters. Here they entered a hallway and walked past several closed doors beyond which Pierce could hear the murmured conversations of families preparing themselves for the day ahead. After two more such hallways, they arrived at a broad stairwell in the center of the house.

The servant made no apology for the darkness, but neither did Pierce require one. They ascended three flights by staircases that grew increasingly well-appointed and richly decorated as they neared the masters' floor. At the top of the final flight of stairs was a carpeted landing, and the young servant led Pierce down another hallway to a door, which he opened to reveal a man sitting at an enormous desk, writing by the light of a double-chimneyed oil lamp.

Pierce had never before seen a lamp of such design, but it did not surprise him to find a novel device on Montgolfier premises. Reflected lamplight glistened from a gold medal lying on the desk. It had an engraving of the *ballon* on it, and Pierce realized it was a royal commemoration of the flight of the sheep.

Etienne Montgolfier, a man in his late thirties with a look of pleasant intensity on his face, wore neither coat nor wig, and Pierce was pleased with the atmosphere of informality. The mill master stood as Pierce entered.

"Monsieur Perce?"

"Good morning, Monsieur." Pierce bowed.

"I am Etienne Montgolfier. This is my brother, Joseph." He gestured toward the corner of the room, where a tall, fit-looking man in shirtsleeves was tinkering with some kind of mechanical wooden device. Pierce realized with a slight start that the device was a simulacrum of a man. The likeness was indifferent, but the limbs appeared ingenious, with joints fashioned of pulleys and small cables. The torso was embellished with rococo carvings, and above that was a head that appeared unnecessary to any purpose but decoration. It had a face painted on it, with an expression Pierce thought rather wistful.

Joseph Montgolfier looked up from his work and nodded.

"I shan't introduce you to Joseph's companion." Etienne laughed. "My brother, you see, is working on a way to replace a three-man vat crew."

Pierce laughed politely. He thought the goal of creating an artificial worker had a certain bizarre wisdom to it, but he could not understand why anyone would want to paint a face on the device. It was just the kind of sentimentality with which human beings so often undermined their best efforts.

Through the window behind the mill master he could see the top of the ravine wall on the other side of the river. The sky was becoming pink as the sun struggled to spill dawn into the valley around the mill. The Montgolfier brothers appeared to have been awake and working for some time.

Etienne studied him by the light of the lamp. "You may sit."

Pierce sat in a chair on the other side of the desk.

Etienne sat as well. Pierce heard a scratching from the vicinity of Joseph. He turned and saw the man had put a small drawing board on his lap and was sketching on it with short, competent strokes of a pencil.

"This will take but a moment," said Etienne calmly.

Joseph finished and brought the sketch over to the desk, where he and Etienne pored over it, looking back at Pierce from time to time as if to check its accuracy. They then proceeded to take various measurements of it with a compass and a ruler.

Pierce had not expected to sit for a sketch.

"Appearance is the first sign of a man's suitability for employment," said Etienne at last. "An irregular physiognomy is often a record of dissolution or animosity."

Joseph returned to the automaton in the corner, and Etienne laid the sketch down on the desk. "I am quite skilled at determining men's ages from their appearance. I would say, Monsieur, that you are twenty-eight."

"Twenty-nine," Pierce corrected. He filed the number away in his mind — that he might remember it if it came up again. "Just last month," he added.

Etienne smiled, obviously pleased with himself.

Pierce actually had no idea how old he was, but he had learned long ago it was best not to be truthful with people about such matters.

"Well then," said Etienne. "I have your endorsement from Monsieur Riffault, and it is impressive. He says he found your advice indispensable in the execution of his

business affairs, and he particularly commended your deal-
ings with the local journeymen's association."

"The journeymen did not want Monsieur Riffault to
install Hollander beaters," said Pierce. "I persuaded them,
however, that increasing production would secure employment for more members of their association." There was, of
course, no Monsieur Riffault. Pierce had written the letter
himself.

"You mean the journeymen's association permitted new
machinery and work procedures?"

"I believe that when a man is hired to work for a
proprietor his loyalty belongs to the proprietor rather than
his craft." Pierce would have elaborated, but Montgolfier
had risen in his excitement and was pacing the room.

"Monsieur Perce, I must tell you that journeymen are
at once the bane and the basis of my life. This mill cannot
make paper without them. Yet as a class their habits are
so irregular and raucous that they keep the place in an
uproar. They are itinerants. We have no way to ensure we
will have the men to produce the paper for orders we have
already taken. We are at their utter mercy."

Pierce now understood what had inspired the Montgolfier brothers to design wooden versions of their vat
workers.

"Not only do these gadabouts disrupt the work, but
they corrupt our apprentices with their habits. They are as
enslaved to their traditions and their festivals as if they
lived in the twelfth century rather than the eighteenth."
Montgolfier walked to the tall window and stood in front of
it, gazing upward toward the coming dawn. After a moment, he spoke to the glass.

"Two years ago, shortly after we brought in a Dutch
machine to grind rags, I promulgated a house rule that the
apprentices were forbidden to participate in the journeymen's rituals. I thought it protection for the younger workers from the dissolution and license practiced by these

rascals." He turned from the window to face Pierce again. "Do you want to know what they did?"

Pierce nodded.

"They left the mill en masse."

Pierce shook his head in sympathetic disbelief.

"And when we hired new men, the journeymen set upon them outside our grounds and battered them. We were unable to staff the mill, and we failed to fill our orders that year."

Pierce suspected it must have been humiliating for the Montgolfiers to default on their orders, although he had no idea what it meant to feel that way.

"Inexcusable." Pierce could hear the distant sounds of work as the mill below them started to awaken.

Etienne turned to look out the window again and mused about his workers. "Nothing is worse than the tyranny workers exercise over their masters, nothing more corrupt and arrogant than this miserable gang of black-guards."

He turned back to face Pierce and seemed to come to himself. "Our workers oppose the Dutch grinding machines. Many of them refuse to operate these machines. I fear some of them are even inclined to destroy them."

Pierce knew he could easily persuade the workers to accept the Dutch grinding machines. It was simply a matter of finding the one who directed the others and persuading him, which could be done with a single feeding. Many times in the past he had pressed his gifts into the service of an employer. He did not mind doing so. He had to feed several times a year in any case.

"Monsieur Perce," said Etienne, "would you be able to advise me on ways of persuading our journeymen to accept the Dutch grinding machines?"

The floor began to hum, and Pierce realized that several floors below them the great mill wheels that spun in the river had been engaged to the mill's machinery. The workday had begun.

"With all due respect, Monsieur." Pierce turned in the chair and gestured toward the mannequin that Joseph Montgolfier was working on. "I think such persuasion will ultimately prove a better course than replacing the workers with automatons."

Through the window behind the mill master, the sun's first scarlet rays emerged from over the ravine wall and poured into the room. Pierce looked down and saw the blood-colored light wash over his arm. It was going to be what people called a beautiful day. He looked up at Etienne Montgolfier, who was shrouded in shadow.

"Then let me ask you another question," said the mill master. "Are you prepared to begin work today?"

Pierce wondered if he would eventually be able to persuade the Montgolfiers to institute night hours for work at the mill. Sunlight never hurt him, but when one sees well in darkness and has no reason to fear it, one comes to prefer it.

"Yes, Monsieur," he said, "today would be excellent."

FIVE

NORMAN was awash in strange feelings. He felt humiliated at the memory of the yellow sticky note on his necktie. He was afraid he might lose his job if he didn't get that check by the end of the day. And seeing how tired Jacqueline looked called up a strange feeling he would call jealousy if he didn't know better. His subordinate was obviously working harder than he, and now she had another meeting scheduled with his supervisor. He knew it was impossible to feel jealous of someone's overwork, but he also had a vague presentiment that he was out of the organizational loop.

Norman stewed about these matters for an hour or so. Finally, he could control himself no longer, and he went to Jacqueline's office to ask about her meeting with Pierce. He tapped on the door. There was no answer.

"Jacqueline?"

There was still no answer.

Norman opened the door. The office was dark. All the shades were drawn and the lights were off. It wasn't as dark as Pierce's office had been, but it was darker than Norman would find comfortable to work in. Jacqueline was sitting at the desk, apparently daydreaming.

"Jacqueline?"

Norman's voice roused her from her reverie.

"Oh, Norman. Hi." Her soft, toneless voice came to him from the gloom.

"Hi."

"Norman, I've been meaning to ask you. Do you think I could move my office to the conference room?"

"Then where would we put the conference room?" said Norman.

"We could move it here," said Jacqueline. "The windows in this room would make a nice atmosphere for departmental meetings, don't you think? I find them a little distracting for getting any work done."

It wasn't like Jacqueline to want to give up an office with windows.

"Sure," he said. "Get Louise to line up some people to move your stuff and reroute the telephones."

"Thanks, Norman. What can I do for you?"

Norman continued standing in the doorway. He didn't want to risk tripping on something if he tried to find a place to sit down. He'd had enough embarrassment for one day. "What's your meeting with Pierce about?"

"He wants a progress report on my business plan."

"Does he want me to be there?"

"He didn't say."

Norman didn't know how to pursue it any further. "Are you OK, Jacqueline?"

"I'm fine, Norman," she said without enthusiasm. "Thanks for asking."

Norman stood there and stared into the darkness stupidly for a moment. When Jacqueline didn't say anything else, he backed out of the doorway and shut the door.

He didn't have time to stew over these things anymore, because it was twenty after two by the time he left Jacqueline. He went to the Controller's Office for his two-thirty appointment.

The Controller, whom Norman hardly knew, was a man nearing retirement. He was known throughout the company for his gruff personality. He was the only manager in the company, besides Pierce, who had a secretary. All the rest of the managers relied on departmental admins.

The Controller's secretary sent Norman into the office,

and Norman stood in front of the man's desk for a moment while he wrote two lines across the bottom of a memo and tossed it into his out-tray. He finally looked up at Norman.

"Yes?"

Norman wondered if the Controller wasn't absent-minded. He had forgotten to invite Norman to sit down.

Norman decided some affiliation was in order. He grabbed a chair, pulled it over beside the man's desk, and sat down in it within a few feet of the Controller's own chair.

The Controller frowned when Norman pulled the chair up beside his desk, but Norman knew that was a particular reaction some people had to attempts at affiliation. It is usually just reflex, and if you continue your efforts to establish contact at a deeper level, most people will eventually accept the connection.

"I need your help," said Norman. "We have to get a bonus check issued this afternoon."

The Controller looked at him suspiciously. "That requires a Certification of Bonus Approval."

"Yes, of course," Norman said as affiliatively as he could, "but Pierce says he wants the check today. We'll have to find a way to streamline the procedure this time."

The Controller looked at Norman, and Norman could see skepticism in his eyes. "*We* don't have to do anything," he said. "I don't think this is my problem at all."

Norman was afraid he wasn't affiliating with the man.

"Of course it's not your problem," said Norman. "I just thought you might want to do something that Pierce was interested in."

"If Pierce wants this check, why didn't he call me to tell me?"

There it was again. The power thing. This man simply resented being out of the loop. Norman could understand the feeling, but he had to get that check. He decided to appeal to the man's sense of fellowship.

"It's a long story," he said. "Just between you and me, I think it boils down to the fact that I was there when he decided he wanted the check written."

"That's not good enough," said the Controller. "Tell me this long story." He looked at his watch. "But make it quick."

Affiliation seemed to be evaporating in the heat of the desire for power. Norman decided to give it one last try and make a play for sympathy.

"I explained our bonus procedures to him," he said, "and he seems to think they are cumbersome and messy. I guess he blames it on me since I was the one who explained it to him. So he told me he wanted the check and he wanted it today."

"Well," said the Controller, "I do know of a procedure for circumventing the Certification of Bonus Approval."

Norman felt a glow of gratification. Affiliation always pays off.

"I'll have to have a memo from Pierce requesting the check," said the Controller.

Norman's heart sank. "You don't trust me?"

"It's not a question of trust," said the Controller. "It's a question of procedure. Just get me the memo and you'll have the check within an hour."

Norman knew he would not be able to move the man beyond this position.

He had no choice but to get him his memo. As he left the Controller's office, it occurred to him that he could write the memo for Pierce's signature. Surely it would satisfy him if all he had to do was sign something.

Back in Human Resources, Cheryl and Louise were still wrapped up in their conversation.

"Look at that stuff," said Cheryl. "The vampire can do anything. He can become a wisp of smoke if he wants."

Norman went into his office, sat down at his computer, and typed up a memo requesting Ackerman's check.

He felt a little small typing up a memo this way, but it would be impossible to ask anyone else to do it without having to explain something of the circumstances of it, and he was too embarrassed to do that. The memo was just two lines, and it took only a minute to write. Norman gave the print command, then went out into the reception area to stand at the printer and wait for it to come out.

"He can become a bat or a wolf," said Cheryl. "He's incredibly strong. He has hypnotic powers over helpless women. Except that in those books you read, sometimes he can do one of those things and sometimes he can't. And there's no rhyme or reason as to when he can turn into a wolf and when he can turn into a puff of smoke. Those books would be a lot more entertaining if they made some effort to obey their own rules."

"What do you mean by rules?" said Louise. "It's not a contest or anything."

As soon as Norman's memo was extruded from the printer, he grabbed it and left with it while it was still warm, so he never heard Cheryl's answer.

At Pierce's office, Norman went to his secretary, a woman in her twenties whom Pierce had inherited from Pressman. She had large eyes and an engaging smile and was given to shirts and blouses that flattered her round breasts. Norman remembered when Pressman hired her, and he had entertained the unworthy thought that Pressman saw most of her qualifications in the area that pushed her shirt out from her chest. She had never had much to say when she was working for Pressman, and Norman had often wondered if her boss hadn't made her uncomfortable with the sort of borderline sexual harassment that some of the old-timers were so skilled at.

But Norman found her surprisingly talkative today.

"It's nice to see you, Norman," she said. "There must be a lot of excitement in Human Resources these days."

Norman agreed that there was indeed considerable excitement and asked if he could see Pierce.

"He's in the executive dining room," she said. "He won't mind being interrupted. He'll be glad of the help."

"Up on the sixth floor?" Norman wondered what kind of help Pierce might want.

"Yes," she said. "Here. Take this." She reached below her desk and pulled out some sort of white folded garment.

Norman took it. "To give to Pierce?"

"To wear," she said.

Norman unfolded it. It was an apron. "I don't understand."

"He's serving lunch to the Maintenance and Janitorial staff," she said.

Norman was appalled. The idea of the company's general manager waiting on its janitors seemed perverse.

Pierce's secretary smiled. "Isn't he the best boss you ever had!" she said. "Until he came here, I didn't even know what kinds of things I'm capable of doing. Did you know I'm now on the Safety Standards Committee and the Administrative Contracts Committee? And I'm no longer a secretary. He made me his assistant."

Norman wondered why he hadn't seen any paperwork on her promotion yet. It wasn't right for managers to promote people without consulting Human Resources. What did Pierce think Human Resources was for, anyway?

But Norman kept his resentments hidden.

He took the elevator to the sixth floor, refusing to put the apron on until he got there and saw for himself.

The executive dining room was filled with diners, men mostly, and most of them were wearing overalls with name patches sewn on the breast. They had elaborate place settings in front of them, several of which still featured plum-colored cloth napkins folded into an attractive fan arrangement. Norman had never been in the executive dining room before, and it struck him that the first time he would get to be here it would be to watch janitors eat.

Pierce, wearing a white apron over his dark suit, was pouring a glass of white wine for the man who emptied Norman's wastebaskets in the evening. Apparently, the man had had several glasses, because he did not appear to be uncomfortable being waited on by the company's top manager.

"Ah, Norman," said Pierce. "Put on your apron and join us."

Norman folded the memo in half lengthwise and slid it into the inside breast pocket of his jacket. He put the apron on.

Pierce handed him a wine bottle. "These people work hard and are very little appreciated for it."

"I need to talk to you," said Norman.

"The former executive team was apparently preparing for some sort of meeting with an elaborate lunch." Pierce turned and moved on to the next janitor and began pouring more wine. "The chef has been working on this meal for days. I decided it should go to someone who might enjoy it."

Norman followed Pierce down the line of diners.

"Norman," said Pierce. "The people on the other side of the table are waiting."

Norman walked around to the other side and began pouring wine. "I have to talk with you, Pierce."

"As soon as we've served everyone, we'll talk," said Pierce.

When they had poured wine for the twelve members of the department, Pierce signaled Norman to come over to him. "We have a few moments before the salad. What can I do for you?"

Norman took out the memo and handed it to his boss. "Would you sign this?"

"What is it?" Pierce took the piece of paper and unfolded it.

"The Controller just needs some backup to issue Ackerman's bonus check." Norman stared at the carpet and wished this were over. He'd never waited table before, and he wasn't sure he liked it.

Pierce left through the kitchen door.

Norman wondered what was supposed to happen now. But a moment later, Pierce reappeared. He was taking his apron off. He tossed it aside and walked toward the door.

"The kitchen staff will take care of the rest," said Pierce. "Come with me, Norman."

Norman hurriedly removed his apron, dropped it on a table in front of the man who picked up the parking lot in the evenings, and followed. Pierce got into the elevator, and Norman stepped in after him. Pierce pressed the button for the fifth floor, Finance. He didn't speak. Norman thought he could hear his own heart beating.

At the fifth floor they got off the elevator, and Pierce started toward the Controller's Office. Norman followed. Pierce did not even stop at the Controller's secretary's desk, although he looked at her and Norman knew he was flashing one of his charming smiles. He went right through the closed door into the Controller's Office. Norman trailed behind him.

The Controller, caught in the act of making an entry on some form, looked up and recognized Pierce. He stood immediately. "Pierce, what a pleasant surprise."

"Clean out your desk," said Pierce.

The man's face went white. "What?"

Norman wanted to plead with Pierce for the man's job, but he was afraid.

"You have sixty seconds," said Pierce, "until I call Security."

"What's this about?" said the Controller.

"It's about your departure," said Pierce. "And you're not using your sixty seconds wisely."

"You can't just fire a man for no reason," said the Controller. "Right, Norman?"

"Forty seconds," said Pierce.

The Controller then turned and grabbed a framed photograph of a dog that stood on his desk. He looked around panic stricken and picked up a coffee mug. Then he pulled the desk drawer open and Norman heard the rattle of loose quarters in the pencil tray as the man retrieved them.

"Time," said Pierce.

"But that wasn't sixty seconds," said the Controller.

"I changed my mind." Pierce reached for the telephone.

The Controller came from behind his desk with his photograph and his coffee mug. "You don't need to do that. I'm going."

He left then, and Norman didn't hear him say goodbye to his secretary. He looked like a man humiliated. He looked the way Norman had felt when Pierce put the yellow sticky note on his necktie.

Norman was afraid to speak.

Pierce turned to him. "Do you think I did that to punish him, Norman?"

Norman nodded.

"You're wrong. I wasn't trying to punish him. I was just trying to fire him. You're the one I was trying to punish, Norman. Why do you think I brought you here to watch?"

Norman felt like he was anchored to the carpet. Some small part of him that maintained a semblance of intelligence wondered why he was not having a fight-flight response, but then realized that neither fight nor flight was possible.

"I think you should come to my meeting with Jacqueline this evening," said Pierce.

Norman didn't feel he had much choice, so when he got back to his office he tried to call Gwen to ask if she would go home early. Gwen's assistant, Carl, told him Gwen was still at lunch with Rod at the Sky Room.

Norman understood that this was the promotion Gwen was expecting. He knew she would want what was left of the afternoon to herself, for parties and celebrations. But Norman was afraid what might happen if he didn't get to the evening meeting with Pierce and Jacqueline.

He asked Carl to give Gwen a message, telling him it was an emergency and that she had to go home early to be with the kids.

Then he tried to relax and prepare himself for the meeting.

* * *

When six o'clock came around, Jacqueline, as if she had been notified that Norman was attending the meeting, appeared in his doorway. She seemed a little less lethargic than she had earlier. She looked no better, but she moved a little more purposefully, as if going to Pierce's office would energize her. She was carrying a leather portfolio, and the two of them walked to the elevator.

The elevator arrived, and they got in. They both reached for the fifth-floor button at the same time, and their hands brushed. Jacqueline's hand felt as cold as stone. The feeling shocked Norman, and he drew away. When he looked at her face, he saw she was staring at him seriously.

"There's nothing for you to be afraid of," she said.

She emphasized the word "you" as if she meant Norman specifically. He should have asked her about it, but he was embarrassed for her that her body temperature had sunk to an inanimate level, and he couldn't think of anything to say.

Norman had always been a little uncomfortable around Jacqueline, but this was different. The inadequacy that she usually made him feel was displaced by something Norman could only characterize as creepiness. It added to the apprehension he already felt about meeting with Pierce.

When they got to Pierce's office, Jacqueline opened the door, and there were no lights on at all.

"Pierce," she said into the darkness, "I brought Norman."

The halogen desk lamp flicked on to reveal Pierce seated behind the desk.

"Ackerman received his bonus check, Norman," said Pierce. "The Assistant Controller cut it for me."

Norman didn't know what to say. He shrugged in the darkness.

"I've often found one of the fastest ways to get action out of an employee is to fire his supervisor," said Pierce. "Sit down."

Norman sat down. He watched Pierce's necktie and shirt front in the circle of light. He heard Jacqueline sit down beside him, but he didn't look at her.

"Ackerman sold a profitable license today." Pierce's voice came from his shadowed face. "It was a critical achievement, and he deserved a bonus for it. When some-body deserves a bonus, I want him to receive it the same day he's earned it. And with the bonus check he will get advice to put the achievement behind him and work on the next one. That's how things are done at Biomethods from now on."

"Do you want me to re-evaluate our procedures for giving bonuses?" said Norman.

"That's not a good use of your time, Norman. Those procedures no longer exist." Pierce's hand pushed a black binder of some sort across the desk toward Jacqueline.

"Now, whenever I think somebody deserves a bonus Jacqueline will write a check."

From the corner of his eye, Norman saw Jacqueline lean forward, pick up the binder, which was actually a large checkbook, and pull it on to her lap.

"On the spot," added Pierce.

"Does Jacqueline report to you now?" said Norman.

"She still reports to you," said Pierce.

"So I'm in charge of bonus checks?" said Norman.

"Of course not," said Pierce.

Norman was afraid the darkness was obscuring his perceptions. How could Jacqueline report to him if she was managing a function he wasn't responsible for?

"You're going to have to learn to live with ambiguity," said Pierce. "I told you that I've come here to tear down walls, and that's what I'm doing."

"Do you want me to track the checks Jacqueline writes for the Controller's office?" said Norman.

"I guess I forgot to tell you there is no more Controller's office," said Pierce.

Norman's mouth went dry, and he felt his throat tightening.

"I fired them all," said Pierce.

Norman was afraid to ask, but he felt he had to know. He had to get enough information to begin calculating his chances of keeping his own job. "What about the Assistant Controller, the one who cut the check for you today?"

"I fired him right after he cut the check," said Pierce.

Norman thought about the poor Assistant Controller, trying to do his best, trying to do what was asked of him, and getting fired for it.

"I don't enjoy this, Norman." There was a gentleness in Pierce's voice that belied his actions. "But people ordinarily don't believe what you are capable of unless you show them."

Norman wished he were home to think about this,

maybe talk it over with Gwen. It occurred to him he might have to leave this job. He might not be able to stomach working for a man like Pierce.

"And you know what I'm capable of now, don't you?" said Pierce.

Norman knew Pierce was capable of firing people on the spot. But he certainly wasn't capable of, say, understanding the Human Resources function. He had nothing to say that would not be rude, so he sat in silence.

"Well," said Pierce, "that's enough philosophy. Let's get to business. I've decided to set up a team to work on Jacqueline's product concept."

Norman looked over at Jacqueline to see how she was taking it. She smiled, but Norman thought it a cool smile, more like the complacency of someone who sees events fulfill a personal prediction than the gratification of somebody who has just changed the course of a multimillion-dollar company.

"I'll need you to process these reassignments." Pierce handed Norman a piece of paper with about two dozen names on it.

When Norman tilted the paper to catch some light from the desk lamp, he recognized some of the names. He might not understand everything Biomethods did, but he was the Manager of Human Resources and he could recognize names. Most of the names on Pierce's list were from the AIDS Department.

"I think some of these people are pretty important to the work on the AIDS cure," he said.

"Not anymore," said Pierce airily. "We're eliminating that department."

Norman probably would have been less surprised if Pierce had told him the company was quitting biotechnology for chicken farming.

"That's the company's most important program." Norman tried not to sound as shocked as he felt.

"It's also symptomatic of this company's problems," said Pierce.

"I don't understand," said Norman.

"What do you know about AIDS, Norman?"

"That it's incurable, and it's probably the worst disease humanity has ever known."

"Very good." Pierce spoke to Norman as if to a particularly slow pupil. "What else?"

"That it's caused by a virus," said Norman.

"And?"

Norman thought. What else was Pierce looking for?

"That it's transmitted mainly by sexual contact and illicit drug use," said Norman.

Pierce smiled. "Bubonic plague is spread by fleas, and yellow fever is spread by mosquitoes. Cholera will get you through contaminated water. Typhoid is transmitted through contaminated food or water. Anthrax is from spores — very easy to inhale them if you're in the wrong place."

"What are you getting at?" Norman was surprised at his own rudeness.

"Do you think there is any market in drugs or vaccines against plague?"

"I don't know," said Norman.

"There isn't," said Pierce. "Plague is almost unknown in the developed world. Eventually it will be gone in the underdeveloped countries as well. It's not being conquered by drugs. We don't see it in this country because we purify the water, we keep the insect population down, and we make it difficult for these diseases to propagate themselves."

"What does this have to do with AIDS?" said Norman.

"AIDS is the most lethal disease humanity has ever known," said Pierce, "but it is also the most easily controllable. How much future can there be in developing a

cure for a disease that can be controlled with public health
measures and education?"

This reasoning seemed particularly cold to Norman,
even coming from Pierce.

"We are re-engineering," said Pierce. "I am going to
make Biomethods a customer-focused company."

Norman did not speak, but waited for him to continue.

"If we're going to be customer-focused," said Pierce, "it
behooves us to choose qualified customers to focus on,
doesn't it?"

Norman nodded. He felt bad about the AIDS project.

"I don't think it's practical to focus on AIDS patients,"
said Pierce. "They aren't the kind of customers we really
want. They die. We put all our effort into building
customer loyalty, and for what?"

"But if we make something that will cure them, they
won't die," said Norman, "and people can be very loyal
when you save their lives."

"That's not true, Norman," said Jacqueline.

Norman looked at her. The light from the desk lamp
was glittering on her bright blue contact lenses, and she
had a kind of demonic look.

"People hate you when you save their lives."

"She's right, Norman," said Pierce. "I've seen a lot of
people die, and I've seen a lot of people live, and the ones
that live have a lot more hatred than the ones that die."

Norman thought this must be some kind of sick joke,
but Pierce's face was in shadows and he couldn't see
whether he was smiling. Even if it was a joke, Norman
didn't feel like laughing. What he felt like doing was checking his files to see how long it had been since he'd updated
his resume.

"Blankenship doesn't hate anybody," said Pierce.
"Jacqueline doesn't hate anybody, do you, Jacqueline?"

The joke was getting sicker and sicker.

"No," said Jacqueline. "I don't hate anybody."

"It hardly matters whether any of us hates anyone," said Pierce. "Do you know how many consumer products are introduced every year?"

"No," said Norman.

"The accepted figure is over twenty thousand," said Pierce. "But only several hundred are actually new products. Most of the rest are existing products with new names or packages. This is a sign of marketing senescence. Modern marketers don't know how to find their customers, so they try to control the other end of the process by modifying the goods they sell to these people they are unable to find. They hope a new name and a new package will cause some excitement or, as they say, create a market niche. Jacqueline's product concept could change everything. If we can predict what a person is likely to buy, we can follow him throughout his life and design new products that precisely address his needs and motivations."

There was a preposterous sort of logic to it, but Norman wasn't prepared to surrender his argument.

"I don't understand about this genetic map," he said. "How can you even make a product out of that?"

"Jacqueline had an idea for that as well," said Pierce. "We will use census data to do test mailings to every adult in the country. Every human being responds to *some* mailing, if only to ask you to stop mailing."

"What will they be responding *to*?" said Norman.

"That doesn't matter," said Pierce. "We'll offer them money if that's what it takes to get a reply. Because, you see, when they reply with the postage-free envelope, most of them will lick the envelope to seal it. Minute traces of saliva will give us the sample we need once we've perfected the mapping test. We will build a database of consumer buying behavior for every single person in the country."

The plan sounded worse than insane to Norman. It sounded megalomaniacal.

"Think of it, Norman," said Pierce. "All the energy,

effort, and expense that goes into redundant and superfluous new product development. This concept could wipe that out completely. Imagine the productivity increase for the entire economy."

Norman had always felt positive toward productivity increases, but he had never thought it would require the elimination of the AIDS Department.

Six

OVER the years, Pierce had learned to arrange his life according to three rules: first, he must never try to sympathize with the feelings of people around him, for he might one day need to feed on them; second, he was never to feed on one to whom he had pledged service; and third, when he fed, he must take care to leave his victim living. The third rule was based more on expediency than compassion, for feeding on a human being unto death created a revenant.

Revenants are insatiable, and in an earlier day on a different continent Pierce had learned what it meant to start a plague of them. Before the plague of revenants had run its course, the beautiful and bustling city of Kilwa was empty of living people. Pierce had never seen such devastation. He learned from that to stake those who had the misfortune to die during one of his feedings, which was the most effective way to keep them from becoming revenants.

At Vidalon-le-Haut, Pierce worked in Etienne Montgolfier's office during the daylight hours and roamed the countryside while the rest of the world slept. He never questioned his failure to sleep, but simply assumed those around him slept in order that he might feed on them more easily. It was his experience that the creatures of the Earth cooperated in this way, whether or not they intended.

His nocturnal travels allowed him to thoroughly study and understand the people and the landscape. He was then able to pick prospects and plan visits to their beds. The entire process was extremely discreet, for Pierce needed to

feed but four times a year, and when he did it correctly he
left his victim with only a vague awareness of it, which the
person would invariably dismiss as a dream — or a night-
mare. From time to time, however, Pierce disobeyed his
rule and surrendered to his gluttony, bleeding his victim to
death. This then required staking and hiding the body. He
would reproach himself for weeks after such a feeding. for
the inconvenience he had caused himself.

Although feeding was vital to his survival, it required
little of his time, and Pierce devoted his energies to helping
direct the work at the Montgolfiers' mill, where he learned
the latest method of fine paper manufacture. It began with
linen rags, which the Montgolfiers purchased from itinerant
rag-and-bone men. Human civilization apparently generated
a limitless supply of rags, and the mill never wanted for
raw materials at a good price. The rags were cooked with
lime and water to clean them and weaken them. Then they
were shredded and ground by blade-bearing drums, called
Hollander beaters in deference to the Dutch origin of the
mechanism, driven by the mill's water turbines.

Reduced to their constituent fibers, the rags were
mixed in large vats with fresh water. The vat men,
attended by their families, mixed in enough water to make
the rags pulpy, but not enough for the mixture to be liquid.
The mixture, in fact, was called "half stuff." Satisfied with
the consistency of the half stuff, a vat man dipped into it
with a rack device called a "deckle." The deckle held a wire
mesh mold. The vat man would scoop out a quantity of
pulp with the deckle and then begin to shake it. The shaking distributed the pulp evenly and caused the fibers to
mesh with one another. It was the part of the process that
required the most skill, for a man must know when the
pulp is even and must not waste himself shaking after the
goal is achieved. A good vat man knows by the appearance
of the pulp when he has shaken just enough. He then
removes the deckle from the vat and lets it dry.

The sheet cohered as it dried, but before it dried too much it had to be laid flat between pads of felt. Stacks of felt and paper sheets were built up and then taken to the mill's great rollers to have the rest of the water pressed out of them. Then the sheets of paper were hung up to dry, a task usually handled by women, who had a touch delicate enough to do it without tearing the sheets before they were finished curing.

Pierce's acquaintance with paper manufacture was brief, however. It was a good year for workers, and they seemed little inclined to either sabotage or licentious behavior. In the spring, Etienne Montgolfier took Pierce to Paris. Paper manufacture, he explained, was dependent upon paper sales, and Paris was where one went to sell fine paper.

Montgolfier kept rooms in the *troisième arrondissement,* and from there he and Pierce would visit nobles of both sword and robe as well as prosperous merchants and bourgeoisie to show them samples of the finest Vidalon writing paper. In the walks and carriage rides from one house to the next, Montgolfier talked ceaselessly of aviation and the next balloon flight, which he and Joseph intended to take place that July. It was the prospect of this flight which held Pierce's interest most effectively, for Etienne Montgolfier had promised Pierce a place in the basket.

One of their visits took Montgolfier and Pierce to the Reveillon wallpaper factory in the *troisième*, where they met Monsieur Reveillon. Montgolfier and Monsieur Reveillon formed an immediate bond of friendship, and they spent the entire afternoon talking about aeronautics, buoyancy, the properties of various gases, and the difficulties of managing workers and itinerant journeymen. Montgolfier forgot to discuss Reveillon's paper needs with him, but came away from the visit with great respect and admiration for a fellow scientist and industrialist.

Montgolfier began to visit the factory owner regularly.

When on the fourth visit Reveillon offered Montgolfier workshop space in his factory, the mill master agreed immediately.

"It will be the perfect place," he later explained to Pierce, "to assemble balloons. My brother Joseph will ship us the paper and the plans from Vidalon, and we will hire men locally to do the work."

"Is there advantage in making the balloons in Paris rather than back in Vidalon?" asked Pierce.

Montgolfier smiled like an indulgent tutor at a quick pupil. "Our work naturally excites interest in aviation among the locals," he said. "There are far more locals in Paris than in Vidalon. We are building a future for aviation by educating a larger number of people."

The Reveillon factory building was as impregnable as the Bastille and, Pierce judged, not quite as airy. To clean the space and install workbenches, he engaged penny-earners. He chose the workers at sunrise in the Place de Grève from the enormous crowd that assembled there seeking employment. He had no basis for choosing them other than their proximity to him when he arrived, and his expectations of them were slight as he marched them to the factory. They were silent as they entered the dark space Monsieur Reveillon had given over at the back of the factory. They behaved as if it were their purpose in life to be herded into dark, windowless buildings.

All morning long Pierce ordered them about in the gloom like so much animate furniture. He sensed their fear of him. It had been his experience that those of lesser education and social refinement often knew implicitly what he was capable of. Every direction, even though he took care to deliver it in a soft, even voice, caused most of them to shrink away and hurry about the work. Pierce thought them fools. If any of them had asked, he might have told them their bodies and their lives were of little interest to him.

At noon, he told them to rest, and all of them except for one or two huddled in the corner of the large, dark room — as far, apparently, as they could get themselves from him. Pierce took his jacket from a hook where he'd left it and started toward Montgolfier's apartment to report to him on their progress. As he stepped into the street, someone called out.

"Monsieur!"

Pierce stopped and turned, and a man was coming from a doorway into the light. He removed his cap as he approached Pierce, but he held it easily at his side and, unlike most of the others, seemed more interested than fearful.

"Excuse me, sir," he said.

"What is it?"

"If you intend to do anything more exacting than rag-and-bone sorting in this building, you may want to improve the illumination."

Pierce suspected the man's tone could be considered insubordinate, but insubordination was a human concept that his self-assurance barred him from experiencing as an affront.

"Do you know about lighting?" said Pierce.

"I have common sense." The man untied a sweat-soaked rag from his throat and used it to wipe some of the dirt from his legs, which were bare from the knee down. He put the rag into a pocket of his patched and threadbare jacket.

Pierce looked down reflexively to see if there was dirt on his own legs, but his silk hose were still quite presentable. "What do you suggest?"

"A series of windows near the roof line." said the man. "At that height they allow the light in without letting people on the street see what you're doing. With shutters, you can close them against all but the most determined intruders."

"Would work like that be expensive?"

"Around a hundred livres for materials and men. It would have been easier if the builder had put the windows in originally, but if you know masonry you know which stones can be removed."

"How do you understand such things?" said Pierce.

"There are many reasons a man might lose membership in his guild."

The guilds, of course, had been abolished eight years before, but Pierce knew that old attitudes lived as long as the people who held them. It was still possible for a guild member to lose his position and be forced into the subterranean world of the penny-earners. As to why such an ostracism could take place and how it was enforced, Pierce knew the man was, one way or another, the victim of some community's hypertrophied moral sense.

"Are you qualified to do this work?" said Pierce.

"I can do it, but the guild would give you trouble if you engaged me."

At the image of a guild making trouble for him, Pierce nearly laughed, but he stopped himself. "I'll ask Monsieur Montgolfier if he wants to have windows."

The man almost smiled, but Pierce could see he'd lost the habit.

Montgolfier did indeed want windows in the workshop and Monsieur Reveillon agreed to the improvement, so Pierce made arrangements for his laborer to direct the work beginning the following day.

The laborer, whose name was Jacques, was waiting at the workshop the next morning when Pierce arrived from the Place de Grève with the day's crew of penny-earners. He had a wooden box full of utensils and devices, which Pierce took to be mason's tools. Jacques used some of these to take measurements around the workshop while the penny-earners were cleaning. From time to time, he borrowed a man to hold the other end of a string or plumb bob. Then he asked for paper from Pierce and sat on a curbstone in the street making sketches.

Once he was satisfied with his sketches, he sent one of the work crew to buy makings for mortar and scaffolding. He ordered the other men around as naturally as if he were born to the work, and Pierce did not interfere.

Pierce watched Jacques' movements — effortless, efficient, and casual — with fascination all day.

When the work day ended at dusk, the workshop space was clean and there was wooden scaffolding in place against the walls.

"We will begin removal of stones tomorrow," said Jacques.

Pierce paid him twice what he paid other members of the crew, then thanked him and sent him home. The laborer took the coins as his due, found his cap and his toolbox, and walked into the street toward the tenement district.

The next day, Pierce told Jacques he wanted him to supervise the work site and to go with him in the mornings to the Place de Grève to gather penny-earners. Jacques simply nodded and attended to the work. His management of the others seemed effortless, and Pierce marveled. It was a rare man who combined the skills and sensibilities of the craftsman with the assurance and persuasiveness needed to make others do his bidding.

There was no longer anything for Pierce to do at the work site, but he was capable of standing in one place and doing nothing for hours. That is what he did over the next few weeks, when he wasn't visiting potential customers with Etienne Montgolfier. He stood and watched Jacques and the penny-earners all day, then repaired to Montgolfier's lodgings in the evening to report on the day's progress.

One day, some weeks later, as the last window was nearing completion, Pierce received a note from Monsieur Montgolfier, who requested that he attend him at his first convenience.

Pierce found Montgolfier in his study.

"Perce," said the mill master, "the balloon paper and the plans will arrive from Joseph tomorrow."

Pierce nodded.

"Have you someone at the workshop you can trust to receive them?"

"Yes," said Pierce. "His name is Jacques."

"Good," said Montgolfier. "I need you with me tomorrow. We shall call on the Bishop of Autun about his paper needs."

"All the way to Autun?"

"A trip to Autun is not necessary," said Montgolfier. "The Bishop lives here in Paris."

The following day found the two at the Bishop's residence. Montgolfier announced himself to the servant and offered his card. The servant, a man of about eighteen years, wore a wig and carried it comfortably. Pierce had noticed that wigs were out of fashion in Paris as a result of the American influence. But the well-to-do would doubtless continue to dress their servants traditionally for another decade or so.

The young man took Montgolfier's card and led the two to an anteroom obviously intended for the Bishop's less important callers. He bowed, then turned and went out the door, apparently to convey the card deep into the interior of the house. Pierce had no difficulty standing at ease in such situations, but Montgolfier, plainly disappointed they were not accommodated in a grander room, paced about, studying the few rather shabby oils in their unornamented frames and tipping chairs to look for maker's marks.

"I rather doubt he will receive me," said Montgolfier to the underside of a chair. "He has never in the past, but I continue to hope I will arrive at a time when he needs to order paper."

Pierce was struck by the randomness of the process. Surely there had to be some way to call on a prospective customer at the time the customer had need of the goods one could offer.

Montgolfier righted the chair, then looked up at Pierce. "Nearly everyone in Paris saw our balloon fly over the Champ de Mars," he said.

Pierce knew the remark was simply candid rather than immodest. He had come to appreciate Etienne Montgolfier as a man of rare honesty and directness.

"I wonder if we might not put the word about that Montgolfier paper is used in the construction of our balloons," continued the mill master.

"Does ballooning prove the quality of paper as a writing medium?" Pierce was somewhat incredulous.

"No," said Etienne, "I suppose not."

Pierce immediately regretted the response. It was surprising how quickly an idea could be killed — faster, even, than a person. He was still trying to think of a way to take back the remark and resurrect the idea when the door latch clicked. The servant stepped into the room as quietly as a deer.

"His Grace will see you now, Monsieur."

They followed the servant down the corridor, Montgolfier's body animated with the enjoyment of an unexpected pleasure.

In a room with a marvelous view of the manicured grounds and garden, they found the Bishop seated at a desk large enough to house one of the poorer families of Paris. He was dressed in a white blouse and cravat and a silk coat the color of spiced wine. His hair was long enough to reach the high collar of his coat, but it did not, because it curled upward in an effect of studied casualness. Pierce thought his attire very much in fashion but decidedly unclerical.

The Bishop stood and walked out from behind the desk. He was wearing silk knee breeches, and he had a club foot, which he managed so deftly that one less

observant than Pierce might never have known. He came
to them and shook Montgolfier's hand like a bourgeois
merchant. Montgolfier was obviously surprised and gratified.

Then the Bishop did the unthinkable. He turned to
Pierce and extended his hand as well.

Pierce felt he had no choice but to grasp the Bishop's
hand. Pierce rarely touched people, as he knew they felt
uncomfortable with the temperature and texture of his
skin, but the Bishop's smile betrayed no hint of discomfort.

"I am Perce," he said. "Secretary to Monsieur Montgolfier."

"A pleasure to meet you, Monsieur," said the Bishop.

Pierce made it a point to be retiring in these meetings, and he was not accustomed to being regarded as
anything more than a tool, like the daybook he carried for
his master. The Bishop radiated grace and civility, and
Pierce was as charmed as he could be by a human being.
He remembered it was said of the Bishop that he could be
receiving a kick in the pants and one would never know it
from the expression on his face. What an extraordinary
man.

The Bishop ushered the two men to a sitting area on
the other side of the room and begged them to sit in the
large, padded chairs next to the fire. He waited until they
were seated before he lowered himself into a third chair,
making a gesture with a handkerchief in his left hand as
he did so. The Bishop did not smell like a snuff taker, and
Pierce wondered if the handkerchief was not merely a bit
of theatrics to distract people from the slight awkwardness
with which the lame man seated himself.

Appearing quite comfortable now, the Bishop grace-
fully slid the handkerchief into the cuff of his jacket and
pushed it up out of sight. "When I was a young man grow-
ing up," he said, "I never dreamed I might live to one day
meet an aviator."

Montgolfier was obviously disarmed by the remark and actually blushed. "It's nothing," he managed.

"Oh, but you are so modest," said the Bishop. "To slip the bonds of gravity; to extend man's exploration to the sky. . . Monsieur, you are the agent of a new era."

It seemed to Pierce a strange reversal when the urbane, fashionable Bishop fawned over the plain, unassuming citizen-scientist.

Montgolfier colored again and was speechless, but the Bishop continued just as if the paper merchant had been responding with the wittiest of remarks.

"You are also a manufacturer of paper, are you not?"

"Well, yes, as a matter of fact."

"As you can imagine, a see runs on paper. Might I dare to dream of using Montgolfier paper to meet its needs? I know this is a great deal to ask. Your mill must be barely able to keep pace with the demand for its products. The public, after all, have the example of your balloons to prove their quality."

When the Bishop reanimated the balloon authentication idea that Pierce had so mercilessly dispatched just moments before, Pierce knew he was indeed in the presence of someone extraordinary. He was struck by the practical quality of the man's wisdom. He knew instinctively that the Bishop had an understanding of relationships Pierce might only aspire to.

"Of course, it would give my family the greatest pleasure to supply your Grace with paper," said Montgolfier. "The demand for it is not so brisk as one might suppose."

The Bishop smiled grandly. "Oh my, how delightful!" Then he seemed to catch himself. "I'm sorry. I did not mean to imply I take delight in anything that might appear to you as misfortune. But if your mill can accommodate a greater business, I would count it as a favor if you were to take the custom of some of my associates and

acquaintances. To act as the instrument of your introduction would considerably enhance my standing in the city."

"But your Grace is too kind," stammered Montgolfier.
"It would be a boon to our business to gain entree to your
acquaintances."

"Please, Monsieur," said the Bishop. "I would consider
it the greatest kindness to me."

"I don't know how I could repay you," said Montgolfier.

"Live a Christian life and be charitable to all," said
the Bishop airily. "The unfortunate are always in need of
our assistance. In my own see of Autun, for example, we
have families living with great misfortunes."

There was silence for a moment, and Pierce could see
Montgolfier forming an idea.

"But your Grace," he said finally, "may I help some of
those families?"

"I would not want to inconvenience you with a journey
to Autun," said the Bishop.

"May I then offer help through your Grace?" said the
mill master.

The Bishop looked surprised by the idea. "I suppose
so." He thought for a moment. "Yes, I would be glad to
accept your help on behalf of the unfortunate families of
Autun." He lapsed into thought again as Montgolfier
waited. Finally he spoke. "I shall prepare for you a list of
my Paris associates and acquaintances who would be interested in purchasing paper. My servant will bring it to you
as soon as I have finished it. If you would make a gift to
the unfortunate, give my servant thirty livres for each
name on the list."

Montgolfier and Pierce left with a substantial order,
and Pierce had rarely seen the mill master so happy.
Whether or not Montgolfier understood what had tran-
spired, it was clear to Pierce that the Bishop had managed
to turn a list of names into a commercial transaction.
Perhaps there might be a future for trading in names.

SEVEN

NORMAN drove home slowly. What was Pierce going to do about withholding when he issued bonus checks? What were the lines of authority in a company where the Assistant Manager of Human Resources wrote bonus checks without clearing them through the Manager of Human Resources? What would happen to the employees being reassigned from the AIDS Department?

In his driveway, he switched off the car's ignition and sat for a long time in the darkness. He felt simultaneously excluded and trapped, and he had no idea how he might make himself a part of the reorganization, or even if he wanted to.

His best hope for dealing with the situation, he thought, was to talk it over with Gwen. She understood organizations and management better than anyone he knew. She would have some insights.

He could see that the lights in the kitchen and the living room were on, and Gwen had left the outside light over the kitchen door burning for him. The bedrooms were dark.

In the kitchen, the air was redolent of cheese, onions, and oregano, and he found a large pizza box on the table. Scrawled across the top of the box in black marker was Norman's home address and beneath that a table of check-boxes with check-marks next to Pepperoni, Extra Cheese, and Onions.

Norman and Gwen had a tacit agreement that they did not bring pizza into their house. They both loved it and they felt that allowing the kids to have it would promote

an unhealthy appetite for it, and they both thought that
denying it to themselves was an appropriate character-
building exercise. He was irritated that Gwen had gone
back on their agreement.

He lifted the lid of the box. There was nothing in it
but a pizza-shaped cardboard and a sheet of greasy, trans-
lucent paper.

Norman found Justin and Megan in the living room
watching television, an infomercial about a patented
job-hunting system. There were three plates on the coffee
table in front of them. Justin's plate and one of the others
were bare. Megan's had a little pile of pizza crusts and
limp onions on it.

"Where's your mother?"

"She's in bed," said Megan.

"Did you have anything besides pizza for dinner?"

"What else is there?" Justin wiped a gout of tomato
sauce from his lip with his thumb.

Norman wondered if maybe he wasn't right. But he
was sorry to see no evidence of Gwen having gotten some
salad into the kids before she let them fill themselves with
pizza.

"I have to go see Mommy," he said.

The bedroom door was closed, and when Norman
opened it he saw it was still dark inside. The odor of pizza
was strong.

He heard sobbing from the vicinity of the bed. He
walked in and switched on the lamp at Gwen's side of the
bed. She was lying there, still fully dressed in her work
clothes. Her eyes were rimmed red, and her face was
streaked with tears. There was a pinhead-sized spot of
orange grease just outside the corner of her mouth.

Norman sat down on the bed beside her. "What's the
matter, sweetheart?"

Gwen pulled herself up enough to push her face into
his chest. She smelled like cheese and pepperoni. "Oh,

Norman. I've been waiting for you to get home. My lunch at the Sky Room, it was—" She was overcome with her weeping, and Norman couldn't understand what she said after that.

"What is it?" he said.

"He told me he's giving Human Resources to that doofus Stevenson." Gwen wailed out the last three words, but Norman understood them well enough.

"The vice presidency?"

"Yes, the vice presidency," she sobbed indignantly. "I didn't get it—" Gwen's breath caught, and she began to stutter with her crying. "—I've b-b-b-been passed over. Rod said I was aggressive. He said he needed team players at the VP level. After lunch, I had to spend the rest of the day acting like everything was all right." The last part seemed to break her down completely. She fell out of his arms and buried her face in the pillow.

Norman sat with Gwen and comforted her for what seemed like days. Her despair seemed like the end of the world. He sat beside her and rubbed her back and made sympathetic noises while she cried. He felt sorry for her; she'd never had a big disappointment before, and she was rather brittle.

He would have preferred being comforted himself, but it obviously wasn't his turn. You can't interrupt somebody else's end of the world with your own, even if that somebody else is your wife — especially if that somebody else is your wife. Besides, what was he going to say? Wait a minute, Gwen. Stop crying for a minute. If you think you've got problems, my boss and my assistant manager are developing a blood test for consumer buying behavior.

It just didn't sound like a real problem.

When she had exhausted herself from sobbing, he made her take off her clothes and climb into bed. He wiped the grease spot from her mouth with his pocket handkerchief. He tucked her in and then left to go see to the children.

They looked up from the screen, where a blow-dried type was explaining the importance of self-confidence to the interview process.

"Is Mommy all right?" said Megan.

"She's had a serious disappointment at work." Norman remembered the bottle of scotch he kept in the uppermost cabinet above the kitchen sink, stored there against occasional moments of suffocation and despair. "You two get ready for bed."

"But it's only eight o'clock," said Justin.

"Yeah, eight o'clock and time for bed."

"But this show isn't over yet."

Norman was going to sit in the kitchen and drink himself into a stupor, and he didn't want his children watching. "You can set the VCR and watch the rest tomorrow. I'm not arguing with you." He started toward the kitchen.

"But Dad—"

Norman stopped and turned around quickly. "Get ready for bed, do you hear me!" He surprised himself with the intensity of his command. He rarely yelled at the kids.

The two of them looked a little scared and then went quietly off to their rooms.

"Don't forget to brush your teeth." Norman called after them. He went into the kitchen. "Not side to side, either," he called into the hallway. "Up on the lowers and down on the uppers." He grabbed the pizza box and tried to fold it over so he could fit it in the trash can. It wouldn't bend properly, and he began to whack it on the floor to soften it up. After half a dozen whacks, he realized he might not be entirely in control of himself. He stood on two corners of the pizza box, reached down and grabbed the opposite two corners, and pulled upward until it gave in the center. He got it folded over and then stood on the fold, bouncing up and down until he had broken the box's spirit. Without being jumped on, the box was probably capable of surviving hundreds of years. It was at least as good a monument to human achievement as the modern corporation.

He threw the box in the trash, retrieved his scotch bottle from the cabinet, and poured three fingers of scotch. He sat down at the kitchen table and began drinking it entirely too quickly.

He wondered if he should go after the kids and supervise them brushing their teeth. He thought about brushing his own teeth. Then he thought about Pierce brushing his teeth. Pierce's teeth. Did he even need to brush them? They looked so expensive they ought to be self-cleaning.

He took a swallow of the scotch, and its warmth made him realize how chilled he'd felt. How are you supposed to deal with it when your boss forms an alliance with your subordinate?

Norman sipped again and remembered how Blankenship had dealt with it when he'd had trouble with his boss. He felt very close to Blankenship because of what he'd been through with him and, in a crazy way, Norman missed him.

The doorbell rang.

It was only a few minutes after eight, so Norman assumed it was the War on Drugs. They had been around the neighborhood a lot in the past couple weeks, getting contributions. Norman had given a little money the day before, wondering what they were going to do with it. What did the War on Drugs need money for? Ammunition?

He left his glass of scotch on the table and dragged himself from his chair. He went to the front door, switched on the outside light, and opened the door.

Norman found himself looking down on a head of white hair. It wasn't the War on Drugs. It was Pierce.

"Norman," said Pierce, "you looked preoccupied when

you left the office. I just wanted to make sure you got home all right."

Norman was torn between fear and anger. If a man isn't safe in his own home, then where?

"May I come in?" said Pierce.

"No." Norman was surprised at his answer. It must have been the scotch talking. He wasn't as rude as that.

Pierce smiled. "That's all right. Most people think it's healthier not to invite me in."

Norman couldn't understand what that was supposed to mean.

"It's not true, though," said Pierce. "It really doesn't matter if I'm invited in or not."

"What do you want?" said Norman.

"Just to reassure you," said Pierce.

"Do I need reassurance?"

"A lot of people lost their jobs today, Norman," said Pierce. "Many more will lose them before this company gets the focus it needs. But you won't be one of them. I need you."

Norman felt flattered that Pierce needed him, but he was suspicious nevertheless.

"I know how to create strategy, Norman, and I know how to organize people. I know how to run a business, and I know how to make money. But I'm not very good at affiliation. Can you understand that?"

"No," said Norman.

"I'm not surprised," said Pierce. "You're good at affiliation. You can't imagine how anyone could lack that skill. But it takes a kind of sympathy I just don't have.

"Keep in mind that whoever is left when I've finished my restructuring is going to be shell-shocked and disaffected. I know. I've been through this before. They are going to need you to help them make sense of the world and to re-establish their sense of community."

"Why do you need me?" said Norman. "Why can't you just behave decently toward the employees?"

"I have no choice over my own nature, Norman." A strange expression came into Pierce's eyes.

"We can each be what we want to be," said Norman, but even as he said it he wasn't certain he believed it.

"You know better than that," said Pierce. "If I handed you a stake right now, could you hammer it through my chest?"

Norman wondered why all of Pierce's images and examples had to be so violently graphic. "Is this another scaffold question?"

"You couldn't," said Pierce. "Because you're not capable of such an act." He looked off into the darkness. "You're not capable of deliberately hurting someone." He looked back at Norman. "And I'm not capable of affiliation. Every person has different capabilities. Bringing them together in the service of some strategy, focusing them on a goal — these are the fundamental tasks of a manager."

Norman wondered how he could end this conversation. "I have to put the kids to bed," he said. Then he regretted saying it, because he thought that letting Pierce know he had kids could strengthen Pierce's position.

"Of course." Pierce smiled, but it was a gentle, civilized smile. "I won't take any more of your time. I just want to remind you that we're on the same team. And nothing's more important than teamwork right now."

Norman felt ashamed. Of course nothing was more important than teamwork. He believed that down to the very core of his being. He just hadn't realized Pierce believed it, too. Pierce was given to violent imagery in his conversation, and he conducted himself somewhat brutally, but they *were* on the same team.

But then Norman realized he didn't know whether or not to feel good about that, so when Pierce left he went back to the kitchen to finish the scotch.

Eight

THE OVERLAND journey to Lyons — site of the balloon launch — took three days, which Etienne Montgolfier decried as injustice. Throughout the first day's coach ride, he held forth on this topic to the various dignitaries he'd invited for the trip.

"It is nothing less than medieval that we should spend three days bumping our way to Lyons," said the mill master. "With a fleet of balloons, such a journey might be accomplished in a day and a half. I envisage balloons one day carrying freight and encouraging commerce from one end of this kingdom to the other."

The guests, mostly aristocrats and government figures, were all quite impressed and hung on his every word. There was a great sense of anticipation among them. And whenever conversation flagged, everyone gazed without prompting at the accompanying wagon bearing the lined crate in which the balloon had been folded and stored, with the great basket lashed on top.

When the party stopped for the night at the first way station and everyone had gone to sleep, Pierce slipped away and roamed the countryside. Dawn found him walking fields, out of sight of the road. Pierce enjoyed the activity of striding across fields and vaulting stone fences. As he gained the brow of a modest hill, he saw something in a broad meadow covering the shallow basin below: a flock of sheep with a small black shape racing around them. A man stood on the slope of the hill upwind of him and did not hear him approach, so Pierce stopped and watched without being noticed.

He recognized the small black shape for a border collie. Running low against the ground, the dog raced to and fro in half circles, nimbly charging wayward sheep in a way that kept the creatures huddled closely together.

Sometimes the dog circled all the way around the flock. By subtle alterations in its path around the sheep, it pushed the skittish flock in different directions. It was thus able to move the flock about the meadow where the man wanted them. These desires the man conveyed by means of whistles, signals with a walking stick, and shouts of "hup, hup!" Although the man's signals were frequent, the flock never traveled in a straight line, tacking about the hillside like a small sailing craft gaining headway against the meadow's incessant wind.

In their work, both the man and the dog appeared to watch the flock, but each attended chiefly to the other, searching apparently for signs of desired and undesired consequences and correcting their actions accordingly. That the man directed the dog's actions was perhaps only an illusion. From Pierce's disinterested vantage point, he could see the two of them had worked their program out together, creating a result greater than the intentions or capabilities of either.

Watching them, Pierce wondered if their work could be considered communication. They obviously tried to make themselves aware of each others' desires, but their actions had none of the intimacy of the intercourse between man and man or between dog and dog, none of the unspoken annotation that gave deep meaning to exchanges between creatures that instinctively understood each other's *raison d'être*. They shared work, but they had no communication, no more than Pierce had communication with human beings. Nevertheless, they herded the sheep competently together, certainly better than either could do alone.

Pierce never once saw the dog bite a sheep, and it seemed to him to accomplish its work of moving the flock away from threats and toward safety with a remarkable economy of effort. It reminded him of his foreman, Jacques, back in Paris.

He was utterly lost in the spectacle when he realized he hadn't heard the man calling to the dog for some moments. He came to himself and saw the man had turned around and was staring at him. Pierce walked down the slope and spoke to the man.

"I was watching you and your dog."

The man leaned on his stick, spat on the ground, and then turned back toward the dog. "Hup!"

Pierce looked over and wondered why the man had called to the dog, who seemed to have the flock well under control.

"Your control over him impresses me, sir," said Pierce.

The man spat again, then spoke without looking at Pierce. "Damned dog grew up with sheep. Thinks they're his pack."

It was a small idea, but most of them were out here in the country. Pierce had not fed since spring, and it was time.

"Hup!" The man wiped his nose on his jacket sleeve, then turned back toward Pierce.

When Pierce took him, he struggled more than most. He flailed at Pierce first with his walking stick and then, after dropping it, with horny, calloused hands. Pierce, intoxicated in the act of feeding, delighted in the creature's impotent blows. He knew then he had no choice but to feed until the man died. It had been a mistake to attack one who was awake, but now he was beyond permitting the man to survive. He surrendered himself to feeding. He lay under the man and let the blood sluice down his throat until he was insensible to everything around him.

He did not know how long he'd been unaware of his surroundings, but he was roused by a strong tugging on his foot. He turned and saw the man's dog had arrived and seized the foot in its mouth. He was worrying it most viciously, although Pierce's boots protected him against its teeth. Pierce sat up and reached for the dog, but it released his foot and backed away. Pierce stood, and the dog circled him at a distance, wary. Whenever he reached toward it, it moved away.

Finally Pierce stooped down, until he was more nearly at the dog's level. The dog watched him cautiously, but when Pierce made no move toward it, it approached more closely. Pierce extended his hand, palm up, to let the dog sniff him. The creature was remarkably alert and intelligent, and Pierce suspected it would be a good companion. He was sure he could make up some story for Montgolfier and that the driver could be induced to let the dog ride on top of the coach.

The dog studied him for a long time, then finally approached to within petting distance. A kind of tenderness such as he had never known welled up in Pierce. The dog brushed his hand with its nose, and Pierce turned his open hand over, then reached out to stroke the dog's brow. Like a sprung trap, the dog clamped his jaws on Pierce's hand. The pain that exploded in the fleshy part below the thumb was remarkable. Pierce tried to draw his hand back, but when he did he brought the dog with it. The creature's grip was unshakable. Fluid welled up around the teeth embedded in the hand, and the dog's eyes stared at Pierce with resolve.

Pierce stood up, and the dog came up with him, making liquid sounds in its throat. Pierce had never been in such pain, and he began to worry that he might not find a way to get the dog off. He finally bent down and picked up the man's walking stick with his other hand. He held the stick as far down as he could. It was impossible to get the momentum for a devastating blow, but he managed to strike the dog hard enough on the side of its head to stun it. It released his hand, dropped to the ground, and took a staggering step.

Before it could run away, Pierce dropped the stick, seized the dog, and broke its neck against the arm of his injured hand. It dropped to the grass and lay still.

Pierce looked down at his injured hand. It throbbed and had begun to discolor. A discharge seeped from its wounds, but the dog had not torn any major elements, and it appeared to be basically sound. He looked at the dog's inert body. He regretted its death. Despite the wounds he suffered from it, he respected the dog and would have liked to keep it, if he'd had the time to persuade it of the advantages of his friendship. But the dog had apparently been too attached to the life it shared with the man. It is quite impossible, he realized, to offer change to a creature determined to kill you. How difficult it is to redirect loyalties!

Pierce used his pocket knife to fashion a stake from the walking stick. He staked the man and buried him and the dog together in a shallow grave.

Then he had to hurry to get back to the way station before the traveling party roused itself.

Pierce's position with Montgolfier had the advantage of invisibility. Montgolfier's invited dignitaries took no more notice of Pierce's injuries than they took of the Roman soldiers who originally graded the road on which their coach rolled so smoothly. Montgolfier himself was too excited and preoccupied with the forthcoming flight to notice, either. Pierce was able to bind his hand with his handkerchief until it would heal, which it did before they reached Lyons. Pierce was a rapid healer.

They arrived in Lyons at the end of the third day. Montgolfier had hired Lyonnaise workers to build a platform to accommodate seating for his guests and for local notables. And while he may have been willing to entrust the running of his Paris workshop to Pierce, he insisted on supervising the unpacking of the balloon himself. On the day of the flight, he started at dawn to build his own fire, with a mixture of green wood, straw, and dried manure, to create the buoyant gas.

"The most efficient lifting is provided by fire with a great deal of smoke," said Montgolfier. "It's the smoke that keeps the craft aloft."

Pierce did not doubt him, but he wished it were otherwise. The fire had a particularly noxious odor and it made his eyes smart.

By the time the audience arrived, having enjoyed their breakfasts, the fire had cast a pall over the entire country-side; the balloon — an ornately decorated bag about the size of a modest château — was inflated with its filthy product and straining at its tethers. Pierce noticed that whatever smoke was not captured by the bag hung low to the ground. He wondered why it should be so instrumental in buoying a balloon upward when alone it could hardly raise itself.

He assumed Montgolfier knew what he was doing, and when his master gave the signal he helped the four guests into the basket and climbed aboard with them.

Montgolfier leaned out of the basket toward the crowd and shouted.

"We ascend for the glory of king and country!"

He signaled for the tethers to be loosed, and Pierce, with the others, felt his insides sink gently but inexorably. He looked down at the basket floor under his feet and realized he was rising rather than sinking. He wondered why his perceptions reversed the sensations.

In moments, they were several hundred feet above the audience and drifting south. Montgolfier himself piloted the vehicle and spoke grandly about the view and the historic event they were part of.

In addition to his sinking feeling, Pierce was struck with the acrid smell and the burning sensation in his eyes, which seemed to be worsening rather than getting better. He did not feel as powerful as he had expected, and he was uncertain as to how much he liked flying.

"Lateral motion is determined by the prevailing winds," Montgolfier explained to his passengers. "If we do not wish to go south, we have but to rise until we find an air current heading in another direction. See those birds over there?"

Pierce did not look with the rest of the passengers where his master was pointing, because he was looking up into the balloon, where he found the source of the distress in his eyes. It was a great deal smokier up there than it had been, because the tough paper bag had apparently been heated beyond its capacity and had caught fire, thus adding to the smoke. Looking through the maw of the balloon at its inside, Pierce could see a small glowing ring in the bag wall near the top.

"Birds can often be used to determine the direction of air currents," said Montgolfier.

"Monsieur," said Pierce.

"Yes, Perce. What is it?"

"The balloon has ignited."

Montgolfier looked up where Pierce was pointing.

"I believe you are right, Perce. Yes, indeed. You are correct."

One of the passengers groaned loudly. Pierce himself felt fear rising in him. He may be one with extraordinary powers, but he knew he was not indestructible, and a fiery death from a great height held no attractions for him.

"No cause for alarm," said Montgolfier. "I've been through this many times. We will begin our descent now."

The mill master's comments calmed the passengers, and in fact everything proceeded the way he had described. It was a modest fire, and it consumed the tough paper bag and its silk envelope slowly. The balloon made a leisurely descent which terminated in a reasonably soft landing. No one was hurt, but Pierce knew that to the people below they had probably looked spectacular coming down amid the smoke and flames.

When the aviators emerged from the wreckage with soot-blackened faces, brushing the fine ash from their clothing, they found themselves seized by locals, some of whom bore them on their shoulders into town while others harnessed themselves to a carriage bearing the balloon's basket like a trophy.

The most notable residents of Lyons competed to entertain and accommodate them. Montgolfier accepted the invitation of a local printer to dinner and lodging. As he and Pierce were preparing themselves for dinner, Pierce asked him about the fire.

"Have you really seen many such fires?"

"Heavens, no," said Montgolfier. "That's the first fire I've ever had. It's the first time I've ever crashed."

"But you told the others—"

Montgolfier held up his hand. "Perce, we must protect aviation from people's fears. The way to do that is to convince them that anything that happens is expected. When they think you have expected events, they believe you are in control of them."

*   *   *

When they got back to Paris, the servant of the Bishop of Autun was waiting for them at their rooms near Louis XV Plaza. Montgolfier went directly back to the study, and Pierce dealt with the servant. The young man had brought the list of the Bishop's friends and acquaintances, and Pierce could tell by its heft that it was a long list. He wondered if Montgolfier could comfortably afford thirty livres for each of the names on it. He did, however, recognize the paper as a product of Vidalon-le-Haut. He admired the Bishop's mastery of detail.

The Bishop's servant followed Pierce when he walked down the corridor toward Montgolfier's study.

Pierce stopped at the door and nodded at the young man to indicate he should wait in the hallway. The young man smiled. Pierce tapped on the door, then entered. But as he was closing the door behind him something caught it, and when he turned he saw it was the young man's hand. The smiling servant slipped into the room.

The young man stepped back and stood against the wall near the doorway, as if trying to create the maximum distance between himself and any activity while yet remaining in the room. Pierce suppressed his irritation and walked over to the desk where Montgolfier was poring over an open account book.

"The Bishop's list." Pierce handed the list across the desk to Montgolfier, who took it and studied it.

It was obviously longer than Montgolfier had anticipated. Strain showed on his face as he counted the names, moving his lips silently as he tapped his finger on each one.

The clock on the mantle ticked once for each finger tap. Nearly a minute went by before Montgolfier looked up.

"Fifty names." Montgolfier managed a smile at the servant. "Please tell your master I am in his debt."

The servant smiled back but made no move to leave his position against the wall, and Pierce wondered if the Bishop had not instructed him to guard Montgolfier.

An awkward silence descended on the room. Montgolfier finally broke it himself.

"Yes?" he said to the servant.

"My master said the Monsieur would be sending a return parcel."

For a moment, Pierce thought Montgolfier might actually feign ignorance of the servant's meaning. But he finally spoke.

"Ah, yes," said Montgolfier. "My gift to the needy families of Autun. Of course."

Pierce thought Montgolfier well served by both his memory and his tedious sense of honor. The society of Paris was the kind of wilderness in which a person does not wish to have enemies, especially enemies as obviously shrewd as the Bishop of Autun.

"I calculate 1,500 livres." Montgolfier reached for a pen and pulled a fresh sheet of Vidalon paper from the desk drawer. He dipped the pen into his inkwell, then wrote precise strokes on the paper. "I have already notified my banker that I would be writing a draft against my account for the Bishop."

Montgolfier finished writing and blotted the paper. He then folded it and held both his candle and sealing-wax stick over it. The sealing wax melted and dripped over the edge of the paper where it laid against itself. He pressed his seal into the small puddle of wax, waved the paper once to cool it, and handed it to Pierce. Pierce handed the paper to the servant, and then helped the young man find his way back to the street.

Pierce returned to Montgolfier's study and found the mill master standing by the window, staring into the street.

"That draft will deplete my reserves." Montgolfier shook his head slowly at the traffic below, then turned to Pierce. "It's a remarkable man who has the ability to turn one's honor to profitable account."

It was the most critical thing Pierce had ever heard Montgolfier say of another person.

Nine

Norman woke up in the morning with the taste of decomposition in his mouth. It was late, and the sun was already up. It glinted redly through the bedroom window while Gwen moved quickly around the room, putting on her shoes, tying her foulard, and slipping into her jacket. Norman hurt as much now as he had when he went to bed, only now he hurt with a headache and a thick, stinking substance wrapped around his tongue.

"Gwen, I have to talk to you." Norman addressed her without facing her. He didn't want to chance she could smell the awful taste in his mouth.

"Can it wait, dear? I'm late again."

"It's pretty important," said Norman.

Gwen stopped her bustling and looked at him. "Norman, I'm sorry, but I was passed over yesterday. If I'm late for work today, it will look like I'm letting it get to me."

"But—" Norman didn't finish, because she'd already left.

He heard her saying good-bye to Justin and Megan. Then he heard the front door close. His head was an anvil — a working anvil, not a decorative one. He dragged himself out of bed. He was surprised that his situation didn't look any more promising by sunlight than it had looked last night in the darkness.

He felt a little better after a shower, a shave, and a mouthwash, and when he got into the kitchen he was pleased to see Gwen had done pretty well with the kids' breakfasts. They were eating cereal, toast, and fruit juice.

His scotch bottle, with two or three drinks left in it, was still sitting on the counter.

The kids seemed a little wary of him. Norman was ashamed, but he tried to act cheerful.

"Watch out for squids at school today." He started to tousle Justin's hair, but the boy moved his head out of reach.

The kids left shortly after that. Norman didn't bother to make himself any breakfast before going to work.

At his office, he found Cheryl at her desk in the reception area.

"There's a PI waiting in your office for you," she said.

Norman wondered why a private detective would be calling on him. Someone investigating Pierce? Norman felt a surge of enthusiasm at the prospect of an ally.

In the chair across from his desk was a severe-looking woman with a heavy demeanor, who did not look up from reading what appeared to be some sort of academic journal. She was wearing a multicolored shawl over a heavy yellow tee shirt and a dark, loose skirt that resembled the peasant garb of some eastern European country. If she was a private detective, she was a very eccentric one. She looked, in fact, like a Biomethods scientist. Then he remembered that PI was Biomethods lingo for *principal* investigator. The company employed a large number of scientists, and although they filled the roles that would be filled in any other company by managers, they refused to be called "managers." The name principal investigator was an academic borrowing that originated in the byzantine culture of government research grants.

"Hello." Norman trudged to his desk and sat down.

The woman looked up. She crossed her legs under the voluminous skirt, and Norman noticed she was wearing Doc Martens.

Occasionally, the infomercials that Norman's son loved so much featured people posing as scientists, and they always wore white lab coats over what appeared to be business clothes. But the only people at Biomethods who wore lab coats habitually were the janitors. The PIs seemed to go to any length to avoid looking either like scientists or business people. They all dressed themselves up as caricatures of graduate students, even the Nobel laureate who sat on Biomethods' board of directors (whose name Norman could never remember). Norman supposed this was some small effort on their part to convince the outside world, or at least themselves, that they had not sold out to commerce by going to work for a private company.

The message indicator was blinking on Norman's telephone. The PI did not bother to introduce herself.

"I'm having trouble with one of my lab technicians," said the PI.

"Disciplinary problems, you mean?"

"It's his attitude," she said.

Attitude. It was never an easy discussion when managers started talking about their subordinates' attitudes.

"What's the matter with his attitude?" said Norman.

"He spills xylene."

Norman wondered if this was an elaboration on the attitude problem or another of the technician's deficiencies.

"Xylene all over the bench. Little pools of it on the floor. Do you know how dangerous xylene is?" The PI looked at Norman as if she didn't expect him to know what xylene was.

Norman, in fact, did not know what xylene was, but it came under his general hazards rule: anything ending in "ene" is a dangerous substance — too dangerous to be left in little pools on the floor.

"Is it part of his job description to handle xylene?"

"Of course," said the PI. "He has to use it to prepare the slides."

"Does he know he shouldn't spill it?"

"Of course. Everybody knows that."

"Did you ever say to him, 'Don't spill xylene.'?"

"Of course not. He should know."

Norman had doubts about the efficacy of "he should know" as a management principle, but years of dealing with Biomethods' PIs had taught him it was well accepted among them. He had never successfully argued any of them out of it.

"First," said Norman, "you will have to issue an Official Probationary Warning to the employee, with a copy to the employee's file. I can help you with the wording if you want."

"Can't you just fire him?"

"I can't fire him," said Norman. "I'm not his supervisor. And in any case, it's far safer and easier on everybody if this is done according to procedure. You wouldn't want to fire him if he didn't spill xylene, right?"

The PI looked uncertain. She smoothed a pleat in her skirt. "I guess not."

"Good," said Norman. "First you send the Official Probationary Warning, which includes a specific description of the employee's primary deficiency. Then you watch to see if the employee's behavior improves. If it doesn't, you send the Second Probationary Warning as soon as the infraction is noted again. This one establishes a deadline for the completion of a goal related to the performance deficiency."

"Goal?"

"Maybe completion of a safety course or something like that," said Norman.

"This seems like a lot to go through just to fire somebody," said the PI.

"As of now," said Norman, "this employee is still on our team. You don't just kick somebody off your team because you feel like it."

"Can't I just send him around here to talk with you?" she said.

"Of course not," said Norman. "An Official Probationary Warning must be in writing, and it must come from you. Would you like me to jot down some notes for you and give you some phrasing for it?"

"I guess so."

"Good," said Norman. Sometimes all you had to do to get people to do things properly was offer to help them out. "I'll have it to you before the end of the day."

She didn't look entirely satisfied, but she thanked him and left. Norman watched the multicolored shawl that covered her back recede through the Human Resources reception area. He hoped she didn't slip on a pool of xylene when she returned to the lab.

The message light was still blinking on the telephone. He picked up the receiver and tapped the RETRIEVE button.

"Norman, I hope it's not inconvenient, but I'll need you to stay a little late tomorrow evening."

The sound of Pierce's voice made Norman's heart sag. He pressed the button to stop the message and sat holding the receiver while he stared at the telephone console, breathing deeply and trying to collect himself.

He thought he'd rather go fire that woman's technician than listen to the rest of the phone message. But he realized Pierce had more control over his well-being than all the PIs at Biomethods put together.

Slowly, like a man calling the IRS about his audit, he entered the code to get into the voice-mail system again.

"Please meet me in my office at seven p.m., if that's convenient," concluded Pierce with the generous politeness the powerful can always afford to show the powerless.

Norman had no idea what Pierce wanted, but he knew it wouldn't make his job either easier or more pleasant.

He sighed and started to call Gwen. He disliked

having to ask her to go home early again, but he felt trapped. He was a little disappointed to get her on the first call. He would have preferred to make his request by voice mail.

"What's the thing you wanted to talk about this morning?"

"I didn't call about that." Norman was not about to use the telephone to tell her about his problems with Pierce. Then a kind of despair rose in him as he realized he was becoming paranoid. Was he worried that somebody might be listening? "I just wanted to ask if you could leave early to be with the kids tomorrow night. I have to stay late."

"Don't worry about it. I'm leaving at five from now on." Gwen's voice sounded its usual competent timbre, but it lacked the edge Norman knew she cultivated for the telephone. Being passed over had somehow wounded her spirit.

He was worried about her, but he didn't see what he could do, so with helplessness settling over his shoulders like a collapsing tent he thanked her and hung up the phone. It was strange how they'd become so distant from each other in such a short time. Maybe it wasn't such a short time. Maybe they'd been distant from the beginning but had simply shared an illusion of closeness. What did he really know about Gwen?

Norman felt that his life had become so bleak so quickly that he must have some kind of hormone imbalance. Surely things weren't as bad as he felt they were. He looked at the pile of papers Cheryl had left in his in-tray. Then he reached over and gathered up the entire stack, put it in the center of his desk blotter, and started to go through it.

Norman could not say that any of the paperwork interested him, but it managed to take his mind off his troubles. Human Resources thrives on detail, and he allowed the details to wash over him and crowd out all other considerations. He gave himself over to a kind of trance induced by an endless succession of memos, requisitions, transmittal forms, and updates. He read them, highlighted them, signed them, sorted them. He crumpled some of them and threw them away, punched holes in some and put them in three-ring binders, filed some in the hanging folders of his lower right-hand desk drawer, stapled some of them to others, attached yellow sticky papers to some with cryptic notes on them. He was barely aware of Cheryl and Louise entering and leaving the office at irregular intervals to drop more papers in the in-tray or scoop the processed ones from the out-tray.

He emerged from his trance when he was aware of his stomach growling. He looked at his watch and saw it was a quarter after twelve. He stood up, stretched, and wandered into the reception area, where he found two empty desks. Cheryl and Louise had apparently gone to lunch without even telling him. Why should they tell him? They probably sensed he was being excluded from the restructuring.

He went down to the company cafeteria and got himself a grilled cheese sandwich and a cup of tea at the counter, then wandered out into the dining room to find a place to sit down.

Cheryl and Louise had a table together, and Norman walked over to it. Their near-empty paper plates had bits of bread crust and catsup-covered plastic knives lying on them. One plate had a gum wrapper on it, and he judged Louise was having her after-lunch chewing gum. They were both working on half-filled paper cups of coffee.

Norman disliked fraternizing with nonexempts, but he felt he needed company and he still hoped he might get the name of that novel from Louise. When he asked to sit down, and they both nodded, he set his plastic tray down on the table and allowed himself to fall heavily into a chair next to Louise.

Nobody said anything, and Norman wondered what kind of conversation he might have interrupted. He bit off a piece of his sandwich and tried to decide whether he should simply ask Louise for the name of the book. He spoke around the melted cheese and bread. "Louise, what's the name of that book you liked so much?"

"Don't get her started, Norman," said Cheryl.

"What's that supposed to mean?" Louise began looking through her purse, and Norman was afraid she was trying to find her hair spray.

"You're going to start talking about vampires again," said Cheryl.

Louise left off her search to look seriously first at Cheryl, then at Norman. "There has to be a reason why every country in the world has stories about revenants."

Norman swallowed the bit of sandwich he was chewing. "What are revenants?"

Cheryl answered before Louise could. "It's vampire jargon. A revenant is a person that comes back from the dead. Revenant folklore is universal to human culture. Why not? There's a natural tendency for bodies to rise from the grave."

"That's what I was talking about." Louise closed her purse, apparently deciding she had a chance at winning the conversation without hair spray.

"But it's not the way Louise means." Cheryl addressed her remarks to Norman. "What do you think started us using coffins to bury our dead? It's because if you bury them without coffins, they tend to work their way to the surface. When they decompose, they bloat. Scavenging animals try to dig them out. There are a lot of natural forces that push corpses back to the surface after they're buried."

"You always do this," said Louise. "You turn a perfectly normal conversation into a lecture."

"Before the days of coffins," lectured Cheryl, "corpses

resurfaced pretty often. People would then try to stake them in their graves to hold them down. That's where all that staking business comes from in the vampire legends."

Louise touched Norman's sleeve. "In one book I read, they opened this grave months and months after the funeral, and they found the body had smooth skin and a mouth full of blood."

Norman stopped eating and pushed aside his plate. He wasn't hungry. He wondered why he had let himself become the center of this conversation.

"It's all part of the decomposition process," said Cheryl. "Look, go ahead and believe in this stuff if you want, but you would do better to recognize that the stories had their start in some fairly simple physical phenomena. And it wasn't until the nineteenth century, when some people saw a way to cash in on the stories, that the vampire acquired the image it has today."

"You think everybody is just out to make a buck," said Louise.

"Aren't they?" Cheryl was looking at Norman.

He shrugged.

"Norman, have you heard any of the rumors?" said Cheryl.

Norman shrugged again.

"They say the company is closing the AIDS project. Is that true?"

In the society of a corporation, knowing something is roughly equivalent to being responsible for it, and Norman felt ashamed for his complicity in closing down the project. "I don't know anything about it," he said.

He got up from the table and took his tray over to the return window. As he was tossing his crumpled napkin into the trash container, it occurred to him that he still hadn't gotten the name of that novel from Louise.

He trudged back to the office.

The afternoon's paperwork was a fog. Norman couldn't

concentrate long enough to read any of it. His hands would pick up a paper, and his eyes would stare at it and go over the words on it, but nothing would come into his head as a result. His mind continually wandered back to the same question: Should he continue working here? The company was abandoning the AIDS project. Pierce had assured him his job was safe, but he faced a threat to the pride he took in working here. Why is everything a decision? Why couldn't a person just live his life and do his work and get on with things?

He called Louise on the telephone and asked her to bring him the file of the technician he'd discussed that morning with the PI. He ordinarily retrieved his own files, but he just didn't feel like getting up from the desk.

A moment later, Louise entered and laid a folder in the center of his desk. He began reading the technician's performance reviews. They were uniformly excellent. The technician's supervisor — the PI Norman had talked with — consistently praised his punctuality, team spirit, and efficiency. She said he contributed a number of ideas for streamlining lab procedures. Norman became absorbed in trying to find the place where the man had begun to go wrong, but he couldn't find it. He felt someone staring at him.

He looked up and saw Jacqueline standing in the doorway. He doubted it was possible, but she looked even more tired than she had the day before.

"Hi, Norman."

"Hi," said Norman. He wondered how late she had worked last night.

"What are you doing?"

"I'm just reviewing an employee file. A PI wants to begin probationary procedures."

Jacqueline drifted into the room like a heavy fog and came around the desk, where she leaned over Norman's shoulder and read along with him about the ideas this technician had contributed.

"Looks like a good employee," she said.

"He looks like a team player," said Norman. "His supervisor tells me he's been spilling xylene on the lab bench. I'm hoping I can persuade her to send him for safety training rather than putting him on probation."

"You're such a caring person, Norman."

She said it so softly that Norman wasn't entirely certain he'd heard it. When he looked up at her, she was staring back at him as if she'd not spoken at all.

"Are you feeling okay?" said Norman. "You look a little pale."

"I'm fine." Jacqueline walked back around the desk and sat fluidly in the chair across from Norman.

They sat there staring at each other without speaking, until a strange voice intruded.

"Excuse me."

Both Jacqueline and Norman turned toward the doorway to see who was there. He was a middle-aged man Norman didn't really know but had seen around the company from time to time. He was obviously nervous, and as soon as Norman looked him in the eye he looked away. He was wearing a lab coat with a radiation badge on the lapel.

"Yes?"

"My boss said to come here to see you." The man fiddled with the radiation badge, as if he were afraid Jacqueline and Norman were emitting gamma rays.

"Why?" said Norman.

"I don't know. She just said I had to come."

Norman realized he was the technician who spilled xylene. The PI had sent him here to be fired, even after Norman's explanations about probation and everything.

"She didn't give you any indication of what it was about?" said Norman.

"No." The man stared at the floor.

Norman was a team player, but he wasn't a lackey for some PI who refused to follow procedures.

"You'll have to go back to her and find out," said Norman. "I have no idea what she wants."

The man shrugged and left.

Norman looked back at Jacqueline. "That's the technician the PI wants to fire. I'm going to call her and tell her how important it is to follow procedures."

"Let me do it, Norman," said Jacqueline.

"It's my problem," said Norman. "I'll handle it."

Jacqueline fixed him with a piercing stare. "I want to take care of it."

She looked so strange that Norman was afraid of what she might do if he refused again. Then he thought how nice it would be to have the whole matter taken care of.

He shrugged. "OK."

TEN

WHEN Pierce and Montgolfier called on the first person whose name graced the Bishop's list, they found a warm reception. The man was a tax farmer named Fleury, and he professed being honored by their visit. He entertained them in a sumptuous office, and Pierce reflected on how lucrative a business tax farming was.

"The entire world knows of your heroism, Monsieur," said the tax farmer to Montgolfier. "The salons are buzzing with talk of the crash at Lyons."

"I'm not a hero, just a scientist," said Montgolfier.

"Nonsense," said Fleury. "They say that at the moment of supreme jeopardy, you were heard to shout, 'I gladly perish for king and country.' They say you fell to Earth in a roar of flames and a cloud of smoke. They say the crash could be heard as far as Marseilles. All of France is relieved you were not taken from us."

It sounded to Pierce like a different crash than the one he'd experienced, and he wondered how they could become so confused about it.

"I practice aviation merely for the glory of France," said Montgolfier.

"The world needs more like you, Monsieur," said the tax farmer. "This country needs more like you. You have no idea, Monsieur, how difficult it is to get people to pay their taxes. Just because it is I and not the crown collecting, they believe they can shirk. But, I ask you, where would this country be if I shirked the payment of my license fees to the crown? No, Monsieur, this country needs some civic responsibility. This country needs more people like you."

"Monsieur is too kind," said Montgolfier. "But the reason I have come is that the Bishop of Autun—"

He stopped, and when Pierce looked at Monsieur Fleury he saw why. The man's face had darkened to a shade it might have taken if Montgolfier had said he'd been in league with Madame Fleury's lover. They sat awkwardly for a moment, and then Fleury regained his composure. His color continued quite dark, but his voice was even and soft.

"I am not interested in anything said or done by the Bishop of Autun," he said. "The man's a scoundrel."

"I meant no offense, Monsieur," said Montgolfier. "I merely wanted to say that I came to inquire about Monsieur's need of fine writing paper. You may be aware that my family manufactures paper."

"Paper?" Monsieur Fleury's color returned to normal.

Montgolfier nodded, apparently judging it best to keep speech at a minimum.

"Paper is the lifeblood of taxation," said Fleury. "Let us see what you have."

Monsieur Fleury was among the most mercurial men Pierce had ever met. Reviewing paper samples seemed to calm him considerably, and Pierce and Montgolfier came away from the visit with an order for several hundred-weight of Vidalon's best.

"Another such visit, Perce," said Montgolfier, "and the Bishop's list of names will have paid for itself."

"Perhaps it is best not to mention the Bishop when making use of his list, however," said Pierce.

In subsequent visits the two discovered that the Bishop's name had extraordinary power over people. The mention of it was enough to excite some people to sing his praises, and to drive others to spit invective. Since it was impossible to tell beforehand which reaction the name would invoke, Montgolfier took Pierce's advice and stopped using it. Nevertheless, those on the list were quite receptive to the idea of buying paper from the "Icarus of Lyons," as Montgolfier had come to be known. Montgolfier remarked to Pierce more than once that the list of names and the destroyed balloon were, together, a better investment than a half dozen Hollander beaters.

*   *   *

Etienne Montgolfier played Icarus of Lyons as long as he could, but the crash turned out to mark the end of his career in aviation. His brother Joseph refused to draw up any more plans for balloons. It was not that he feared for anyone's safety, but he had become interested in a project with Monsieur Lavoisier to create a device for equalizing temperatures, and he could not be persuaded to work on anything else.

Without Joseph's designs, Etienne was no longer an aviator, and he gradually lost the interest of his best Parisian customers.

With sales weakening, the mill master looked for new sources of revenue. When he conceived a plan to obtain a government grant for the development of Dutch papermaking practices at Vidalon, Pierce decided it was time to take his leave.

It sometimes appeared to Pierce that it was his fate to be continually disappointed in human beings. In the past, he had pledged his service to those he thought were masters of political, social, or intellectual power. And in time, each had either sacrificed his power or come to grief, or both.

He had yet to find a person who could remain faithful to power. Human beings seemed incapable of discerning when they had it and when they lacked it, much less of using it carefully. They were always using it to provoke overmatched enemies, spending it too recklessly, or giving

it up when it became too difficult to keep. Vlad of
Wallachia, Charles I of England, Gaileo Galilei — each
had, in his turn, disappointed him.

Pierce felt there was a great deal remaining for him
to learn about power, but he knew one thing for certain.
Little, if any, of it resided in institutions. Pierce had lived
long enough to see untold governments, religions, noble
families, and social orders pass away. As far as he had
come to understand it, mankind had but one permanent
institution: commerce.

He knew instinctively that there was no better place
to learn commerce than at the feet of the Bishop of Autun.
Had not this man, after all, managed to create a commercial transaction from nothing more than a list of names?

To Pierce's surprise, the Bishop actually remembered
him and received him warmly. More than that, he seemed
extraordinarily pleased to hear of Pierce's availability and
offered him a position as his secretary starting immediately.

"Is there no one in the position now?" said Pierce.

"Just Fleury," said the Bishop. "He is the son of a
local tax farmer, and I have taken him on as a favor to his
mother, but he has not been working out."

The Bishop then sent for Fleury and, in Pierce's presence, dismissed him. As with everything the Bishop did, he
was both considerate and civilized about it, such that by
the time the interview was over it would seem to any
onlooker, and no doubt to young Fleury himself, that
Fleury had resigned. The young man left the room to
retrieve his personal things, and Pierce thought that,
except for having two good legs, he looked remarkably like
a young version of the Bishop.

*   *   *

As the Bishop's secretary, Pierce spent all of the work day
with him, but it was not a particularly fatiguing regime.
The Bishop typically rose at noon, breakfasted until one
o'clock, answered correspondence until two, and then
visited various parishes and society figures until four. In
the late afternoon, the Bishop was always home and
usually attended by his tailor or his barber. He dictated
plans to Pierce as he was being shaved or fitted. The
Bishop was an expert husbandman in the loam of human
society. He planted seeds, he fostered growth, he harvested.

His network of friends, lovers, and associates was
impressive. Most of the letters Pierce prepared for his
employer (and the man's correspondence was voluminous)
consisted of carefully crafted requests for favors or calls on
obligations due him. Pierce marveled at the power available
to one who masters relationships.

Nothing in the routine touched on Autun, and Pierce
learned that, but for his ceremonial consecration at the
cathedral there, the Bishop had never been to the place.
He rather marveled that, in absentia, the Bishop was able
to discharge his clerical duties so effectively, for he was
widely regarded as the most able bishop in all of France.

Nevertheless, the Bishop's moment-to-moment style of
life was exceedingly agreeable, and Pierce was surprised to
find how easily he fell into it. There was always a fire in
the hearth, the furniture was comfortable, the staff moved
discreetly and behaved solicitously. Even the clothing was
pleasing. The Bishop gave Pierce all his old clothing and
the services of his tailor to alter it. Pierce, therefore,
acquired new clothing at the same remarkable rate at
which the Bishop did. None of the clothing was particularly
clerical, of course. Except for ceremonial occasions, the
Bishop's only sartorial concession to his office was a cross,
elegant in its simplicity, which he wore on a chain about
his neck and generally kept tucked into his waistcoat. It

was a life altogether sufficiently comfortable to be described as sybaritic by the uncharitable.

The Bishop was as well educated as he was shrewd, and as his confidant, companion, and amanuensis Pierce had some of the most thought-provoking and stimulating conversations he had ever had. He also met virtually every significant figure of Parisian society. He absorbed the best and the worst thinking of the day on the country's problems: the evils of tax farming and the salt monopoly, the degraded condition of the public treasury, the chronic shortages and the concomitant grain riots.

Although these issues were the object of a great deal of public attention, French society seemed powerless to deal with them. Gradually, the country worked itself into a state of general want and misery, which devastated the poor and created discomfort for the rich. Commerce shrank, and in the Paris salons frequented by the Bishop Pierce overheard conversations that led him to believe the Montgolfier mill was slipping into difficulties.

By 1789, pamphlets and broadsides began to appear in general distribution on the streets of Paris, but they were printed on cheap, low-grade paper, and Pierce thought they would do little to improve the demand for the kind of paper the Montgolfier mill specialized in. One day after the soldiers frog-marched one of the broadsides' distributors off in the direction of the prison, Pierce picked up a broadside from the cobblestones in Louis XV Plaza. He found it to be full of nonsense purporting to advise the King on the management of the public debt by nationalizing the tax structure. He discarded it. Pierce found taxes extremely dreary.

He remembered his service to King Charles, who had believed a king rules by divine right. The King had thought that belief was enough to make it so. Worse than that, he could not restrain himself from saying it loud, even as he demanded more money from the country's reluctant taxpayers. Only the separation of his head from his body by the headsman's axe had silenced him on the subject.

*   *   *

On a morning in April, the servant brought with the Bishop's breakfast the news that a wallpaper factory had been burned out by a mob in the *troisième arrondissement*. There was only one wallpaper factory in the *troisième*, and Pierce asked the Bishop if he could have the time free to go there.

It was a cold day for April, but the air was warm on the street, especially near the Reveillon factory. Pierce joined a crowd around the smoking stone husk. The heavy walls were scorched, and daylight came through the windows, because the building no longer had a roof. Charred beams protruded here and there, and it looked to Pierce as if the ashes inside had accumulated to a depth of two feet or more. Bits of ash still floated around him and the air was acrid. Except for the heavy stone walls, the destruction had been quite complete. Nothing remained of either the factory work areas or the Reveillon residence that had occupied the floor above. Pierce wondered if Etienne Montgolfier had lost anything in the fire.

The crowd was mostly locals, and they all seemed to be dressed shabbily. Pierce realized there was a great deal of want in the city, perhaps more than he had understood before. An old man with an unkempt beard and an unsavory smell was standing next to him.

"Is Monsieur Reveillon all right?" said Pierce to the old man.

"The whole family was in the house." The man laughed. "But don't worry. There's plenty more rich ones and aristos left. It's good to see Parisian rats get their dinner roasted once in a while."

"Why did this happen?" said Pierce. He knew there

was a great deal of social unrest abroad in the land, and
he expected to hear an accusation against Monsieur Reveillon for exploiting his workers or something of the sort. But
that was not the reason the shabby man gave.

"They did guild work in there, and they had no guild,"
said the man.

Pierce had thought that the guilds were at least
partly, and perhaps mostly, to blame for the conditions of
the common people. It was the guilds that kept people from
gainful employment, as in the case of Jacques. It was the
guilds that both controlled and stifled commerce. It struck
him as odd that poor people would fight so hard to protect
them. It reminded him of the dog he'd had to kill near
Lyons, except the poor were not quite as well fed.

He turned and worked his way back out through the
crowd. At its edge he found Etienne Montgolfier. The mill
master stood with a small portfolio cradled in one arm and
was apparently sketching something on a sheet of paper
against it. He was working hard and did not seem to notice
Pierce as he approached. Pierce waited quietly until he had
stopped for a moment. Montgolfier looked up and saw him.

"Perce."

"Monsieur," said Pierce. "I am sorry about your
friend."

"Reveillon was an honorable man and a scientist," said
Montgolfier. "Did you know he paid his workers a third
higher than anyone else in the city? I think that is why
they burned him. They were jealous of his workers."

Pierce reflected on how delicately one must balance in
order to control people. Push them too hard, and they rise
up to demand your head, as they'd done to King Charles.
Do them favors, and they rise up to burn you out, as
they'd done to Monsieur Reveillon. Somehow, you must
keep them both fearful and well-fed, like the border collie
with the sheep.

"Did anything happen to Jacques?" said Pierce.

"I don't know." Montgolfier added a few lines to his sketch, then closed his portfolio on the paper. "I haven't seen him since yesterday."

Pierce wondered if his protégé had survived, for he assumed Jacques was the cause of the mob's attack.

Montgolfier looked around. "Paris has become a dangerous place, Perce. I am going back to Vidalon." He nodded, then turned to leave.

"Will you fly again, Monsieur?"

Montgolfier stopped and turned back to face Pierce. He appeared to consider the question for a moment, then he shook his head resolutely. "How can I be certain the Earth would be here when I returned?"

ELEVEN

NORMAN pulled his car into the driveway and switched off the ignition. The outside light by the kitchen door was on, and it comforted him that his family was expecting him home. He felt extremely uncomfortable. In the matter of the technician, he had the distinct feeling that Jacqueline had usurped something from him rather than taking an onerous matter off his hands. He hoped he'd be able to talk with Gwen about some of this stuff tonight.

He got out of the car and dragged himself into the house.

The remnants of a take-out dinner were piled up on the counter in the kitchen. His scotch bottle was still there, and it still had two or three drinks in the bottom. He inspected the take-out containers. There wasn't anything left, just spots of some indeterminate sauce in one of them. He wasn't hungry anyway.

He poured the remains from the scotch bottle into a glass and walked out into the living room. The sight of his family all sitting together on the sofa restored him somewhat.

Gwen was between Justin and Megan. She had an arm around each of them, and the three of them were watching television. It looked like the same infomercial Justin and Megan had been watching last night. The same blow-dried personal growth specialist was explaining the importance of self-confidence to a studio audience of people who looked like they needed it.

Norman's family hadn't heard him enter, but Justin looked up and saw him when he came up beside the sofa.

"Hi, Dad."

Then Gwen and Megan looked up and greeted him as well. Gwen looked at the glass of scotch in his hand, and her expression became overcast for a moment, but then he could almost see the effort behind her eyes as she brightened and smiled at him.

"Hi, sweetheart," he said.

Gwen pointed the remote at the television, paused the tape, and set the control on the coffee table. She held her arms out toward him.

Norman sidled in front of the coffee table and bent over to kiss Gwen. He hugged her one-handed, holding his scotch in the other. He gave Megan a one-handed hug, then tousled Justin's hair.

"What have you squids been up to?"

The kids summarized their days at school much more briefly than he would have liked, then Justin picked up the remote and started the tape again.

Norman wanted to sit down on the sofa with them, but he needed to finish his scotch and he felt a little ashamed of the way he probably smelled as a result of the liquor. So he sat down in his reclining chair. It creaked as he pushed up and back to stretch himself out. Then he watched the tape with them while he sipped at his drink.

The infomercial seemed particularly stupid. They were pushing some kind of kit with forms and notebooks and software. It was designed to help you prepare a resume, write a cover letter, and prepare for a job interview. It didn't seem to provide anything that wasn't readily available to a person born with the rudiments of human intelligence.

"Hey, Justin," said Norman, "isn't anybody doing spray-on hair or steak knives this evening?"

"Norman," said Gwen. "I thought it would be useful

for the children to see this. It's never too soon to learn how to prepare a good resume."

It occurred to Norman that maybe he should pay attention.

When the tape was over, Norman's glass was empty, and he had managed to retain nothing about how to prepare a good resume. It was time for the kids to go to bed. Norman and Gwen went from room to room and tucked them in the way they had a few nights ago, but Norman felt like he was sharing tucking-in responsibilities with a stranger. It's surprising how you can live with someone for so long and then suddenly realize she is just as lonely inside her own skin as you are inside yours. He wondered if he should try to talk with her about Blankenship.

Norman decided he should keep their conversation on office affairs. He asked her about her day.

"It was just fine," she said. "You finished that whole bottle of scotch, didn't you?"

Norman shrugged. "I've got problems at work. Bad problems."

It did not seem to surprise her. "Does it have to do with the turnaround?"

"Yeah, but probably not the way you think."

"You aren't being laid off, are you?"

"I don't think so. But I'm getting spooked by this re-engineering thing."

"Re-engineering?" It was the kind of talk Gwen loved most in the world.

"I want to get your insight on this guy Pierce," said Norman.

"Is he really re-engineering the company?"

"I don't know. I guess so."

"Tell me, Norman." Gwen was excited now. "Did he start with a blank sheet of paper like the experts say you're supposed to do?"

"Yes, as a matter of fact," said Norman. "But that's not what I need to tell you about."

"Is he eliminating all the departments? What's he going to do about compliance if he eliminates Human Resources?"

"I don't know," said Norman. "I'm mostly concerned about what he's doing to our product line."

"Product line? What do you care about the product line? You're the Human Resources manager."

It sounded very similar to something Norman had said to Jacqueline a few days before. That seemed a lifetime ago now.

"I don't know." Nothing seemed to make any sense to Norman, and he felt like he was under incredible pressure.

"Take off your clothes and get in bed." Gwen began taking her own clothes off. "You're as tense as a knot. You have to get relaxed."

Before he knew what was happening, Norman was stripped and on the bed, and Gwen, also naked, was astride him with her hips undulating as she worked herself down on to his erection. She put her hands on his shoulders, leaned forward, and began rocking rhythmically. It was not a position from which he could easily explain what was happening at the office. He found, in fact, that he couldn't think about anything except what was happening in his groin.

After they had both climaxed, he fell into a deep and dreamless sleep.

*   *   *

In the morning, when Norman arrived at Human Resources, Louise was sitting at her desk in a fog of hairspray, staring at a pile of memos.

"Good morning," said Norman. "Is anything going on this morning?"

"It's strange here today, Norman," said Louise. "No

calls. Nobody coming in. And this morning, I found these on my desk." She scooped up the pile of memos and handed them to Norman.

Norman took them and looked through them. They were termination memos, dozens of them. They were all signed by Jacqueline.

"What's going on, Norman?"

"I don't know anything about it," said Norman. The remark had become a kind of slogan for him.

"You're the department head, and they need your approval," said Louise.

It was difficult to tell if she was just making an observation or accusing him of something.

He went into his office and sat down at his desk to wonder again what was going on.

He heard Cheryl come in and strike up a conversation with Louise.

"It's just the same old story," said Cheryl. "Only it seems a little different because it's set in a small town in Maine."

"That's why it works so well," said Louise. "You don't expect vampires in a small town. You don't expect a little town in Maine to have unspeakable evil."

Unspeakable evil. Norman had never really thought about the idea of evil before, much less unspeakable evil. The company had a chance to make some kind of progress on AIDS, and Pierce was throwing it away to do something with direct marketing. Was that evil? Was it unspeakable evil? It occurred to Norman that people threw around the idea of evil without really looking at it. He got up from his desk and walked over and stood beside his doorway so he could hear better.

"Oh, come on, Louise," said Cheryl. "Don't you think it's just a little bit simple-minded? They screw around sharpening baseball bats until dusk before they go looking for the vampire, and then they're surprised when he catches them in the dark. Why is it that the only character with any sense is the vampire?"

"Excuse me." Norman stepped through the doorway to the outer office.

They both turned to look at him.

"Have either of you seen Jacqueline today?"

"Not yet," said Cheryl.

"Why did they sharpen baseball bats?" said Norman.

"They make good stakes," said Louise. "A nice handle, and the end is flattened, so it's easier to hit with the hammer."

"Did they get him?" said Norman. "Did they stake him? In the book, I mean."

Cheryl rolled her eyes, as if she'd been trapped in a roomful of fools.

"Yeah, they got the big one," said Louise. "But then it was too dark, and they had to let the rest go."

"What happened then?"

"Everybody in the whole town became vampires, except for a man and a boy, who got away."

"The whole town?"

"Yeah," said Louise. "The man came back later and burned it down."

"Oh, God," said Cheryl in disgust.

"In the daytime," added Louise.

Norman went into his office and sat down behind his desk to think about all this. Sharpened baseball bats. A whole town becoming vampires. Norman decided he wasn't interested in the novel about the vampire rock star in New Orleans anymore.

Norman had never had problems at work before, and he didn't quite know how to deal with this. He had always been a team player. He'd never been particularly visible, but he'd made his contribution and had taken pride in the company, because he'd known he was part of it. But the company wasn't the same now. Pierce talked about teamwork, but he really didn't seem to care about it. Look at the way he was making Jacqueline into a star.

Norman heard some kind of commotion going on in the outer office, but he tried not to pay attention. He looked at the pile of termination memos Jacqueline had written up. He knew he should start processing them. He took the top one. What if he refused to process them? Would these people still lose their jobs?

"Norman?"

He looked up and saw Louise standing in the doorway.

"Yes?"

"Do you have the employee file for a technician in the Arthritis Department?"

Norman remembered the technician who spilled xylene. His file was still in the pending tray. He reached over and grabbed the manila folder. "Yes."

"May I have it?" said Louise. "The police want it."

"The police?"

Two people materialized behind Louise. She gave a little jump and turned toward them. Then she stepped aside, and they both moved into the doorway. One was a youngish woman who looked like a bank clerk and the other an older man who looked like the guy at the department store that they call out of the office to come approve your check.

"That's all right," the man said to Louise. "We'll look at it in here." He nodded toward Norman. "We should talk with him anyway."

The two of them walked into the office, and the woman who looked like a bank clerk closed the door behind them.

The man lowered himself into a chair while the woman took the technician's file. She laid it open on top of a filing cabinet and examined it standing up.

"I'm Detective Riordan," said the man.

He could have used some of the spray-on hair Norman

had seen on television the other day. He had a lined but hearty-looking face. His stomach was just beginning to protrude over his belt. The Police Department apparently didn't have an employee fitness program.

"That's Detective Capuano," said Riordan.

At the mention of her name, the bank clerk looked up from the file. She had dark hair and the pale eyes of a character actress whose name Norman couldn't remember. He judged her to be in her late thirties. She didn't speak but went back to the folder.

"What's this about?" said Norman.

"One of your employees ran into a problem on the job," said Riordan. He took a small notebook from his coat pocket, then reached inside his coat and brought out a ballpoint pen that appeared to have a Police Department emblem on the pocket clip. Norman recognized the pen as the kind organizations give as gifts and incentives. He received glossy catalogs for that kind of stuff all the time.

"You mean with a supervisor?" said Norman.

"That's what we're trying to find out." Riordan twisted the pen to expose the point. "The secretary down there found him in the lab this morning. He bled to death."

Norman was stunned. "Admin," he said.

"What?"

"You said secretary. I'm sure you're talking about an admin."

Riordan made a little waving gesture with the hand holding the pen, as if he thought this unimportant.

"You're the personnel manager here, right?"

"Human Resources," said Norman.

"What?"

"I'm the Manager of Human Resources."

Riordan waved again.

Norman wondered if the man thought nothing important.

"Did he cut himself?" said Norman.

"Who?"

"The technician," said Norman. "You said he bled to death."

"It wasn't a shaving cut or anything like that," said Riordan. "Puncture wounds. In the neck. Do you know anybody who had it in for this guy?"

"His supervisor wanted to fire him," said Norman, "but she didn't seem to me to be homicidal."

Riordan made a note in his notebook. "Anybody else?"

"The guy was a pretty good employee," said Detective Capuano from over the file cabinet. "Why would his supervisor want to fire him?"

"I don't know," said Norman. "Jacqueline was checking into it."

"Jacqueline?" said Riordan. "Who's that?"

"She's the Assistant Manager of Human Resources," said Norman. But he knew when he said it that Jacqueline was much more than that. There just didn't seem to be any way to bring that up in a way the police would understand. She's the company's rising star, handpicked by our general manager, and she looks like she's suffering from a world-class case of fatigue.

"Can we talk to her?" said Riordan.

"She's not in right now," said Norman. "She's been coming in late these days."

"Oh?" Riordan wrote in his notebook. "Is it usual for her to come in late?"

"I don't know what that has to do with anything," said Norman.

"When you have a possible homicide," said Riordan, "you look for any sort of change in people's behavior. Sometimes it leads to something. Sometimes it doesn't. When do you expect Jacqueline?"

"I don't know," said Norman.

Riordan stood up. "Here's my card." He handed

Norman a business card. "Tell her I want to talk with her."
He turned to Detective Capuano. "Anything?"

She shrugged.

"Bring the file along, then," he said.

The two left. Norman got up and followed them out of
his office. Cheryl and Louise stopped their conversation and
turned to watch the police officers as they left.

"Norman," said Cheryl. "You'll have to process another
death."

Norman shrugged and walked back into his office. He
was thinking about Jacqueline. He wanted to ask her if
she'd seen the technician yesterday.

But she didn't come in for the rest of the day.

* * *

When it was time for his meeting, Norman went up to
Pierce's office.

The fifth floor was, of course, deserted when he got
there. He went to Pierce's office and tapped on the door.
The door opened.

"Come in, Norman."

Jacqueline was sitting on the corner of Pierce's desk.
Norman wasn't surprised. He was beyond being surprised
by anything.

She was wearing a power suit, but it looked like it
badly needed cleaning and pressing, and he wondered if it
wasn't the same one he'd seen her wearing yesterday. She
was holding a stack of memos and reading them very
quickly, although Norman thought the light too dim for
comfortable reading.

"Pierce is running a little late." Jacqueline didn't look
up from her memos.

"I needed to see you, anyway," said Norman.

Jacqueline didn't answer, but continued to read her
memos.

"The police were here, and they want to talk with you."

Jacqueline didn't say anything.

"They think that technician was murdered," said Norman.

"What technician is that?" said Jacqueline.

"The one we were talking about yesterday," said Norman. "The one in the Arthritis Department that the PI wanted to fire."

"I'm sure he'll be missed," said Jacqueline.

Norman had no idea how to respond to such callousness.

He tried to be casual, and he wandered around Pierce's office just as if it weren't dark. He studied the spines of the financial binders on the shelves, examined the furniture, felt the drapes at the window. It occurred to him that Pierce's office had almost no personal items. There were no mementoes, no pictures, none of the debris that enlivened the offices and cubicles of the rest of the company's employees. There weren't even any little yellow sticky notes on his computer monitor.

Norman's wandering took him to the other side of the room, near Pierce's desk, at the opposite corner from where Jacqueline sat. There was a letter opener there. It was not standard company issue, and Norman seized on it as a clue to Pierce's character. When he looked at it carefully, he thought it might not be a letter opener, but then why would a manager, even one as strange as Pierce, keep a stiletto on his desk? The handle was wrapped with a leather strip and had a pommel in the shape of a human head. Norman couldn't see all that well in the gloom, but the face looked like it had a wistful expression. Norman picked the implement up and felt the blade. Yes, it was a letter opener; the blade had a dull point and was about seven inches long, but it had no edge. It was comfortable and well-balanced, like a well-designed weapon. Norman thought he could sit at a desk and open letters with it all day long.

"It's a baselard," said Jacqueline. "It dates from the eighteenth century. Pierce is very fond of the eighteenth century."

Jacqueline's demonstration of her intimacy with the company's power center had the effect that Norman judged she wanted it to have. He felt excluded. He laid the letter opener on the desk. "I thought it was a letter opener."

"It is." Jacqueline continued to read her memos. "Not very much other use for a dagger in an office."

Norman knew what Jacqueline was doing to him, and still he let her do it. He let her make him feel small. She had a direct connection to the company power center, and he stood out on the fringes. Now he was expected to suck up to her as if she were more powerful than he was. But then, she was. Norman couldn't stop himself from doing just what he was expected to do.

"How are you, Jacqueline?" he said solicitously.

Jacqueline looked up. She was not wearing her contact lenses, and a cold fire burned in her dark eyes so that when she looked at him it hardly mattered how dim the light was. "How do you think?"

"I didn't mean to anger you," said Norman.

"I'm not angry," said Jacqueline. "I don't get angry anymore."

That was as much as Norman knew about sucking up. What should he say next? He had asked after her health. He wasn't going to ask about her family, because he knew she lived alone and didn't have any. He had to face it. Since they had no personal basis for conversation, he would have to keep it focused on work. He gestured at the memos in her hand.

"Important stuff?" he said.

Jacqueline shrugged. Norman had never seen her make that gesture before, and he didn't know she was capable of it. But when she did it, she gave it a fluid grace that he rather admired. All of her movements, in fact, had become much more graceful than the deliberate, impatient Jacqueline he'd known before. She looked at him over the stack of memos in her hand. "Who knows what's important anymore?"

Norman thought she intended the question to be rhetorical, but she invested it with a kind of inhuman despair, and it moved him. He remembered that they had worked together for a couple years and that she had been the best supervisor he'd ever seen.

"Are you all right, Jacqueline?"

"Of course I'm all right. Why do you ask?"

"To be perfectly frank," said Norman, "you haven't looked well. And your behavior has changed. You used to be the best manager I'd ever worked with, but lately you don't seem to follow the procedures very well."

Norman thought he detected a softening of the cold fire in her eyes, as if she were somehow pleased about something. But then the hardness returned, and she looked a little like an ice sculpture in a badly pressed business suit.

"I'm a much better manager now, Norman." Jacqueline dropped the memos on to Pierce's desk with a flopping noise. "We have a great deal of work to do here, and we can't let the procedures get in our way." She stopped talking and looked toward the doorway. "Hello, Pierce."

Norman was startled. Pierce stood in the doorway.

"Jacqueline." Pierce stepped into the office beside Norman. "I have to talk with you. Wait in the other room, and I will be along in a moment."

Jacqueline glided off the desk and out the door.

Norman watched Jacqueline until she vanished into the shadows, and when he turned back around, Pierce was seating himself at his desk.

"Norman, I'm glad to see you."

"Pierce, do you think Jacqueline is all right? She seems overtired."

"When people start leaving the organization, the ones who are left bear the burden of additional work. Jacqueline knows the risks." Pierce looked at him. He must have smiled, because his white teeth glinted out of the shadows. "I've been doing this for a long time, Norman. I know how to deal with these things."

"Doing what?" said Norman.

"Never mind," said Pierce. "We have work to take care of."

"Wait a minute, Pierce." Norman was surprised at his own assertiveness. "Jacqueline has been acting strange ever since that meeting here in your office last week. What's going on?"

"We are re-engineering, Norman. It's not an easy process. You don't win a battle without killing people."

"Who said anything about battles?" said Norman. "Or killing people?"

"It was just a metaphor," said Pierce airily. "Like you."

Norman recognized that Pierce was sharing something with him, but he didn't know what. He strained to extract some meaning from the comment.

Pierce seemed to interpret the puzzlement on Norman's face. "You're a metaphor for a border collie."

The room was silent, and Norman wondered if he was expected to reply. But he couldn't. Somewhere along the way, his relationship with Pierce had changed to where there was no real communication between them. Norman couldn't understand at least half of his boss's conversation. He'd never really grasped the idea of the metaphor anyway. He was absent the day they discussed it in high school.

Pierce spoke softly.

"I'm sorry, Norman. I didn't mean to trouble you with

an idea. I had forgotten what a problem those are for you."
His voice was warm and sympathetic, the way Norman
might talk to Justin.

"Pierce," said Norman, "I need to know what's going
on. I need to know what you want from me. Nobody's
following procedures. Departments are being eliminated.
People are dying. The police are investigating."

Norman realized it made no sense to drag the technician's death into all this, but everything seemed to be
falling apart at once and it all seemed related. Pierce,
apparently, would have none of it.

"Do you blame me for that poor man's death?"

"Of course not," said Norman. He didn't know what to
think about anything. He was overwhelmed with a feeling
of despair. "I'm sorry. I guess the pressure is getting to
me."

"Deal with it, Norman," said Pierce. "I told you how
much I need you. If you fold under the pressure, a lot of
people in this company are going to be lost. These people
need you. They need you to be alert, to protect them from
danger. That's what I mean when I compare you to a
border collie."

Norman didn't know if he should feel flattered. But
frustration corroded his restraint. "You shouldn't be closing
the AIDS project, Pierce. It was the best thing about this
company."

Pierce did not reply for a moment. When he spoke
again, his tone seemed more businesslike, less expansive.
"There's no cure for AIDS, Norman. There never will be."

He said it with such authority that Norman was
gripped by the feeling that it must be true. "How do you
know that?" he said at last.

Pierce ignored the question. "I've sent some termination memos to your office," he said. "I need you to implement them."

"You want me to fire people?"

"Yes."

"That's not part of my job, Pierce. I'm a Human Resources manager. I don't fire people."

"You do now," said Pierce. "I've already fired the rest of the department heads. That leaves you."

"But I didn't get termination memos for any department heads." Norman felt like he was in a boat and he'd lost the oars.

"I would think you'd know by now," said Pierce, "that I often move faster than paperwork."

Norman didn't know what to say.

The two of them sat in silence for a while. Pierce finally spoke.

"I've considered the matter, and I think you can handle nine terminations a day. You could probably do more if you handled them as a group situation, but we don't want to be inhuman about this, do we?"

TWELVE

THE GOVERNMENT was nearing bankruptcy that year. Shortly after the burning of the Reveillon factory, the King finally agreed to convene the Estates General in hopes he might discover a new method of taxation. Pierce remembered Charles I and the Short Parliament. Were kings incapable of learning from one another?

The Bishop, seized by an excess of civic-mindedness, declared his intention to stand for election to the First Estate, the clerical assembly. Pierce had no regard for politics, but he knew that if anyone could make a success of it the Bishop could. He helped the Bishop write his election mandate, which promised a great deal of political change that it never specified. As men who got their living from a corporation nearly two thousand years old, the priests who voted for him were extremely conservative.

Although the Bishop won his election, he never had the opportunity to propose any changes to his colleagues in the First Estate. Directly after the elections, the Third Estate — the popular assembly — challenged both the other estates and the King for primacy and almost immediately slipped into a power struggle with them, which resulted in its reconstituting itself as the National Assembly. Most thought this was simply an attempt by the bourgeois politicians of the Third Estate to embarrass the aristocrats and churchmen of the other two estates. But the situation seemed more serious than that when the National Assembly announced that it was determined to write a constitution for France and make Louis XVI a constitutional monarch.

The standoff between the National Assembly and the other two estates did not last long. Almost immediately, constitution-minded members of the First and Second Estates began resigning and declaring themselves members of the National Assembly. Street conversation each day brought additional names of crossers-over, and the newspapers and pamphlets published lists of them weekly.

The Bishop watched the national mood carefully while considering when to cross over. He finally joined the National Assembly a week before the First Estate was dissolved: soon enough to share in the heroism of resigning the establishment and late enough to be assured the establishment was not going to survive. Pierce marveled at his timing, and he realized the Bishop was the first person he had ever met who actually understood political power.

But no one understood power on the streets of Paris. In July, a mob of about six hundred people — with dozens of defecting soldiers — stormed and took possession of the Bastille, liberating seven aging, nearly forgotten prisoners and taking possession of the city's largest powder magazine. The people startled even themselves with the force of their strategy, and the nation at once understood that the genie of a people's army, now freed, could never be rebottled.

The countryside was convulsed with random, sporadic killings and attacks that touched every village and town in the kingdom. Roving bands of brigands were said to be devastating the countryside. Far fewer people were killed by brigands than by their neighbors and friends, but the public is more apt to fear what it cannot see than what it can, and the fear of random violence stalked the landscape.

Pierce had seen communicable insanity before — the Albigensian Crusade, the witch hunts of 1580, the Thirty Years' War — but he had assumed it was a peculiarity of Christianity. This was the first secular insanity he had ever seen. He forgot about the Bishop's political career and took himself into the country to watch this strange spec-ta-cle. He walked by night from town to town, mixing himself in crowds by day. He saw stonings, hangings, and brawls, and he could not remember a time when the air had been so thick with suspicion. It was a delight.

His first feeding that summer was on the teenaged daughter of a baker. He was tired of peasants and beggars, and he chose her because her father was prosperous enough to give her a bedroom to herself. He followed her to mass for each of two days and then crept to her bed in the middle of the night. He was skilled in approaching peo-ple, and he knew he had not made a sound crossing the room from the window where he'd entered. Nevertheless, she sat up as soon as he touched the bed.

"Are you an angel?" she said.

Pierce knew it was too dark for her to see his face, but he did not let his voice betray his amusement. "Yes," he said.

"I knew you would come," she said. "I have prayed for you every day. Have you come to bless me?"

"Are you worthy of this blessing?" he said.

"Oh yes, yes," she said.

"Even if it hurts a little?"

"Yes."

So Pierce put his right hand on her forehead and gently tilted her face away from him. He covered her mouth with his left hand and bit into the vessel of her neck. He need not have covered her mouth, for she did not cry out. Pierce marveled at her self-control. She must have wanted his blessing a great deal. Her blood was sweet with the purity of youth, and he surrendered to the temptation of drinking until her heart could no longer pump it into his mouth.

When he roused himself near dawn, he found she was pale and lifeless. He heard stirring in another part of the house and footsteps approaching the door. He had to flee

before anyone entered, and he did not take the time to
stake her. As he was stealing across the garden below her
window, he heard the bellow of a father's grief.

The next day, rumors of a strange sickness swept
through the town's narrow streets. She was a popular
young woman, and before the end of the week there was
an imposing funeral mass with a great deal of public grief.
The father instructed his journeymen to bake loaves of
bread for free distribution to the citizenry in her memory.
Free bread, of course, added to her popularity, and the
town's sadness was acute.

Grief and sadness, however, were swept away the day
after the funeral mass, when the girl rose from the grave
and began attacking townspeople in their beds.

The parish priest formed a *posse comitatus* of the
bravest men in the town, and they hunted the girl down
before sunset the day after the first attacks. Pierce
followed at the fringes of the group, amused at the urgency
with which the townsmen felt they had to run her down
before dusk.

They finally chased her to the town square in front of
the church and surrounded her. She was wearing her white
burial gown, although it was no longer entirely white.
Brown spots at the collar revealed that she had not been a
very dainty feeder. And she had torn a foot or more of
material from the hem of the gown to facilitate movement.
The circle of townsmen, armed with clubs and pikes, closed
in. When they were close enough, two of them dropped
their weapons and seized her arms. She snapped at them
viciously. She drew blood on one of the men, and he made
as if to strike her, but the priest stopped him.

"We are not here to punish," he said. "We are here
only to drive out the evil that has animated this body."

So the two men wrestled her to the pavement and
held her down while the priest kneeled beside her. He
chanted a prayer in Latin as he placed the point of a

wooden stake against her chest. Pierce did not understand the prayer very well. It had been centuries since he had last spoken Latin. With the first blow of the priest's mallet on the stake, the revenant gave out a scream that shook the stained glass windows of the church. She did not bleed greatly, for she had fed only twice and incompletely. The second blow left her still. The priest stood slowly and led the townspeople in a prayer. Pierce prayed along with them in order not to be conspicuous. He need not have worried. The townspeople were so absorbed with their deliverance from the revenant that they noticed nothing but their own prayers.

They left her in the town square that night as a sign to other revenants who might be about, and the people returned to their homes before dark. Pierce went to the church late that night and saw a light burning in the rectory. He understood the priest was still awake, so he called on him.

His name was Father Henri, and his quarters were spare, although Pierce suspected he chose rather than endured the life of the religious Spartan. His small room was furnished with nothing more than a chair and a cot.

Father Henri gave Pierce the chair while he sat on the cot.

Pierce found himself staring at the only decoration in the room — a crucifix on the wall above the cot. It brought to mind a bit of folklore: some people thought that one such as Pierce would shrink from the sight of a crucifix. He looked at the thing. It was indifferent workmanship, and he wondered how the idea got started that such an object could harm him. Perhaps if it were sharpened at one end and driven forcefully into his body, it could slow him down. But surely a pike would be more effective for such a task. Father Henri shook Pierce from his musings with a question.

"What can I do for you, Monsieur Perce?"

"Today you said it was necessary to drive the evil from that girl's body. I want to know how to recognize evil."

"Anyone with faith can recognize evil," said Father Henri.

"I want to know how to recognize faith," said Pierce.

Father Henri looked at him quizzically.

"Have you no faith, Monsieur Perce?"

"I do not know," said Pierce. "I am innocent of spiritual experience."

A light came into Father Henri's eyes, as if he were an explorer at the edge of one of America's uncharted wildernesses. He told Pierce a long story about the religious experience that caused him to enter God's service.

Henri (for he had not been ordained then) had been a soldier enlisted in a brigade under the command of the Comte de Rochambeau. His unit served in America, and when they were in a place called Rhode Island the general pledged them to the service of the American general, George Washington. Despite language differences, they worked closely with the American soldiers and enjoyed good fellowship with them on a rapid march southward from Rhode Island to a place called Yorktown in Virginia.

At Yorktown, the combined American and French forces laid siege to the British forces under General Cornwallis.

"If you have never seen service in a siege, Monsieur," said Father Henri, "it is more work than you can readily imagine. The besieging army builds a city in every way comparable to the place under siege: fortifications, gun emplacements, and a large, active population of soldiers and camp followers. It would be an admirable effort were it not dedicated to violence and destruction."

Henri's unit was one of the most active in the siege operation, for he was a sapper. These are the men whose task it is to undermine enemy fortifications, which they do by working in trenches, called saps, that approach the enemy in zigzag patterns. The general strategy is to dig trenches that extend as closely as possible to the enemy positions and then find a way to breach the position, usually by tunneling in and placing explosive charges.

"It is difficult and dangerous work," said Father Henri, "and we did not have enough men to work all the saps the generals thought necessary, so we asked the Americans for additional. As I say, it is difficult and dangerous work, and we were not entirely surprised that none of the American soldiers wanted to join us. They sent us slaves."

At first there was a great deal of grumbling among the French about the slaves. The Americans, after all, were the ones who were supposed to benefit most from the operation. It was ingracious of them not to put themselves at risk. But the grumbling stopped when the French came to know the slaves, with whom they got along famously. There is not a great deal of difference, after all, between being a soldier and being a slave. Both are owned, or are as good as owned, by someone with the power of life and death over them. Both are flogged when their masters believe they are moving too slowly.

Working side by side with them, the French soldiers taught the slaves to speak French. The slaves taught the French to sing strange and mournful songs in a language they'd never heard before. Henri became close to one of the slaves, a strong young man named Cicero. It was not a name he'd chosen for himself, he explained in his broken French, but one given to him. Prodded to it, he told Henri his real name, but Henri could not pronounce it and continued to call him Cicero. Cicero was kept manacled at night with his fellows, but Henri sometimes sneaked into their quarters and brought them extra rations and grog, which they enjoyed immensely. One night, under the influence of a generous quantity of grog, Cicero and Henri traded flogging stories.

Cicero's floggings sounded no worse than those endured by Henri, except there were far more of them. Cicero judged he had been flogged a hundred times or more in his life. Even with the grog working on him, however, Cicero could not be induced to express any bitterness about the way he'd been treated. Henri judged this was not because he felt charitable toward his oppressors, but because he did not trust Henri's white face enough to confess what he felt.

Henri was one of half a dozen men assigned to work on a tunnel in the soft earth of Virginia. They would dig several feet forward, shore up the excavation with timbers, and then dig some more. It was a small, close excavation, and every twenty feet they had to make an opening in the ceiling to the ground above in order to freshen the air. Somebody, whether it was the engineer who designed the work or the carpenter who cut the supports in a nearby forest, made an error, and when they had advanced the excavation fifty feet they had a collapse.

"There were three slaves in the tunnel at the time," said Father Henri. "They were, in fact, the only men there. I was the first to arrive after the collapse, and I found Cicero, barely alive, with a great timber across his chest. He could not speak. He lived but a moment longer, in any case, with his head in my hands. At the moment of his death a wonderful feeling of peace overtook me, and I felt his soul brush past me."

"And that was your religious experience?" said Pierce.

"Yes," said Father Henri.

Pierce had of course held many a head at the moment of death and had never felt anything of the kind. Religious experience, apparently, requires some sort of susceptibility. Pierce thought he probably lacked this susceptibility.

"Will I not be able to recognize evil if I have never had a religious experience?" he said.

"Evil is the absence of good," said Father Henri, "just as darkness is the absence of light. If you can recognize light, you can recognize darkness. If you can recognize good, you can recognize evil."

Pierce thought Father Henri reasoned like a child, and apparently his opinion showed on his face.

Father Henri's eyes widened. "You have been sent to me by Satan, haven't you?"

"I have seen more things than you can imagine," said Pierce. "But I have never seen Satan."

The priest clutched the rosary at his waist.

Pierce was afraid he might start praying, and he was not sure he could bear the tedium. So although he had no need, he fed on Father Henri.

The priest struggled like an animal. Pierce wasn't prepared for such a fight and in subduing him made a much greater wound than he expected, opening an artery. As Father Henri's blood squirted from the torn vessel in his neck and life slipped away from him, he hissed a prayer.

"Father, protect the soul of your servant from this evil one."

Pierce took offense. Would Father Henri consider him evil if he understood that Pierce had no choice in what he was? Father Henri died before he could discuss it with him.

He looked around at Father Henri's room. It was a monstrous sight. The cot and the chair were overturned, the crucifix had been knocked off the wall, and there was blood everywhere, a great deal of it on Pierce himself. Pierce had always been fastidious about feeding and derived no particular pleasure from spilling blood. He had to break up Father Henri's chair to get the makings of a stake, which he then forced through the priest's chest. The man would have made a very poor revenant.

When he finally left Father Henri's room and walked into the dark street below, he was troubled by Father Henri and his prayer. Had the man actually expected help from some supernatural source?

Pierce was chagrined, perhaps even ashamed, at his own behavior. First he had allowed a victim to become a revenant, and then he had fed when he had no need. Had he been affected by the mood of the countryside, by this Great Fear? Had he allowed these people to excite him into disobeying his own rules?

It was as close as Pierce had ever come to having moral qualms, and he found the feeling to be uncomfortable. He had never consulted a human being for advice before, but it occurred to him there was someone who might be of help. He returned to Paris to call on the Bishop of Autun.

The Bishop was delighted to see him and invited him to sit at his old desk while they talked, as if a season had not passed since they had seen each other.

"Perce, I was afraid I had lost you. I have searched everywhere for you."

"I have been in the country," said Pierce.

"It does not look like it has done very much for your health," said the Bishop. "You look tired."

Pierce felt tired.

"The political situation has considerably changed. I am working with Monsieur Mirabeau to prepare a plan for asserting the authority of the National Assembly over the Church and then assuming ownership of its property. We are going to put the priests on salary."

Pierce wondered if Father Henri would have considered that good news.

"Your Grace," he said, "could you explain to me what makes a creature evil?"

"Why, Perce, what a strange question." The Bishop toyed with the cross on the chain about his neck. Then he illuminated the room with one of his gracious smiles. "I hope you have not given birth to a religious conscience, Perce."

Pierce did not think there was much danger of that, but he was still rather haunted by the experience of Father Henri.

"I'll not be a bishop for very much longer, Perce, and I feel I can be candid with you about my beliefs." The Bishop tucked the cross into his waistcoat. "Let me tell you about myself. I am the second son in my family, and as such I have no prospect of inheritance. Those in my position have but two choices: the military or the Church. I do not fancy violent behavior of any sort, so I chose the Church. The Church is a good career for an intelligent and educated man.

"I know that many of my contemporaries consider me opportunistic and without conscience. But I have values. I believe in decency, and I believe a man is responsible for what he does.

"Every man has an uncivilized creature inside him, waiting for the opportunity to emerge. Some men lack the self-control to keep the creature inside — these make up the criminal classes. But even decent people find it difficult to keep the creature under restraint in times of stress, such as war, famine, or political turmoil. Rather than own the uncivilized part of themselves, men — decent or otherwise — ascribe their behavior to something they call evil.

"The idea of evil, then, to the extent it diverts our attention from controlling our behavior, promotes evil. It is one of those interesting puzzles, is it not?"

Pierce did not like puzzles as much as the Bishop did.

"Does that answer your question?" said the Bishop.

"Frankly, no," said Pierce.

"A story, then," said the Bishop. "In the year 1212, a

peasant boy, Stephen of Cloyes, organized a Holy Crusade. He was joined by children from all over the country, and thousands of them marched to Marseilles. Two notables of the time, Hugh the Iron and William of Posqueres, offered the children boats to take them to the Holy Land. Once all the children were aboard the boats, Hugh and William took them to Africa and sold them into slavery."

Pierce happened to have known Hugh the Iron and thought him a perfectly ordinary man.

"I dare say," said the Bishop, "that three-quarters of humanity, in possession of the boats and confronted with the opportunity, would have done the same thing as Hugh and William did. But they don't want to believe it of themselves. So they say such an act is evil, and hope that by avoiding evil they will not do such a thing, or if they do they will not be blamed for it, because they only did it, after all, under the spell of evil."

It was an explanation that caused everything to make sense. Evil was a human construct, developed by people to help them avoid responsibility for their behavior. Pierce thought it a shame the Bishop was leaving the Church. He had so much to teach humanity.

"Now I understand, your Grace," said Pierce. "Thank you."

"Now then, Perce," said the Bishop. "It will devolve upon me to consecrate the new Constitutional Church. I intend that to be my last act as a priest. I will resign my bishopric and stand for election in the department of Paris. I will need a good secretary, and I want you with me in this endeavor.

"I expect to be excommunicated directly," continued the Bishop. "You need not address me as 'your Grace' any longer. From now on, I will be known by my family name, Talleyrand."

"I am afraid I have not yet been able to nurture an

interest in politics, Monsieur Talleyrand," said Pierce. "I will not accept your offer."

"That's a shame," said Talleyrand. "You were the best secretary I've ever seen. Intelligent and indefatigable."

Pierce wished him good fortune and took his leave. When he got back out on the street, it was night, and he decided to feed.

Thirteen

When he got home, Norman tried to talk with Gwen about the whole mess. They sat cross-legged on their bed in the dark, and he tried to tell her everything that had happened since Friday. But he didn't want to seem melodramatic about it, and he left out a lot of details. He never mentioned how Pierce always kept his office dark and that Jacqueline had begun to resemble something out of a labor camp. And it didn't seem entirely relevant that one of the technicians had been murdered.

As he rendered the story without these elements, however, he became acutely aware that he was describing a pretty typical corporate reorganization. He was not surprised when Gwen reacted unsympathetically. Her voice came to him from across the bed in the darkness.

"I'm not sure I understand what the problem is, dear."

"He's making me fire several dozen people," said Norman.

"Did you expect the company to be re-engineered without some terminations?"

"The way it's being handled seems so brutal," said Norman.

"Corporations are always brutal, dear. You know that." Gwen reached over and patted his leg in the darkness. "They take all the loyalty you care to give, and then when they're ready to fill a vice presidency they promote a doofus like Stevenson. That's the way it is.

"You just have to take your lumps," she added, "until you get the chance to give some."

Then she kissed him perfunctorily, and they got under

the covers to go to sleep. But Norman couldn't sleep, and after lying in bed for ten or fifteen minutes he got back out, put on a bathrobe, and went out into the living room. He picked up *Anatomy of a Turnaround*, sat down in his recliner, and read a chapter about what the author called the "cash-out artist."

> You must not confuse the turnaround specialist with the cash-out artist. Although the latter often poses as the former, the two could hardly be more different. The turnaround specialist seeks to strengthen a business, while the cash-out artist seeks only to liquidate anything of value. The cash-out artist is a plunderer. He will strip and sell the assets of a business down to the carpeting. If labor regulations allowed it and the price justified the effort, he would probably even bleed the employees.

Of course the author was just making a macabre joke, but the coincidence was not lost on Norman. Had Pierce bled that poor technician? Norman knew it was an unworthy thought about his boss, but he could not get it out of his head. Pierce talked about killing people to win battles, and then this technician turns up dead. But what possible profit could there be in killing a technician? What would motivate that kind of behavior?

Norman slept dreamlessly in his chair that night. He woke up before the sun came up, looked at his watch, and saw it was time to start getting ready for work. As a result of being in a strange position all night, he felt as if he'd been stapled to the chair. His future looked as bleak as it had ever looked to him. He had to drag himself to Biomethods again and spend another day dealing with police detectives, trying to avoid unpleasant surprises, and firing people.

Firing people.

When Norman got to work, he went straight to Pierce's office. Pierce's assistant sent him right in to see him. Norman was grateful he didn't have to serve anybody lunch in order to talk with him.

He found his boss in the darkened office with the desk lamp shining its circle of light on the desk.

"Norman," he said, "have you scheduled any of those termination interviews yet?"

"Not quite yet," said Norman. "I wanted to talk with you about it first."

"There's nothing to talk about," said Pierce. "You have to get started. The sooner you do it, the easier it will be on the people who are being terminated. Besides, we will be bringing in new hires. I have to get the others out of here."

"Why are we bringing in new hires if we're terminating people?" said Norman.

"I appreciate your concern for these people, Norman," said Pierce. "So I want you to try to look at it from their point of view. The way it looks to them, we are turning the world upside down. We are making this company into a place where things will fall up and where the ground will be above them rather than below. I have worked with people and organizations a long time, and I can guarantee that nearly all of them will never adjust to this 'upside-down' world. It is kinder to terminate them."

Norman hardly saw any of this as kindness.

"That's why I have chosen you to handle it, Norman," said Pierce. "You are, by nature, a kind person.

"Jacqueline," continued Pierce, "will be conducting the interviews to hire the new employees at the same time you are terminating the old ones."

Norman felt like quitting right then and there, but what Pierce said next made him reconsider.

"If you don't terminate these people, Norman, then I'll assign Jacqueline to do it. She has asked for the assignment. She seems to think she would enjoy it."

The idea of Jacqueline firing all those people and

enjoying it was discomforting. Norman had hired many of those people himself. He could not in good conscience consign them to Jacqueline's amusement. It might be the last thing he would do for this company, but he decided he would have to do all the terminations. He was still a team player.

When Norman got to Human Resources, Jacqueline was already there. She looked no better than she had the night before, and her power suit had begun to smell a little. She followed him into his office.

"You're here early," said Norman.

"Lots of work to do," she said. "I've been nailing down the details. I think it's best I should interview candidates in the conference room, don't you?"

Norman wondered if she was going to make these poor people submit to interviews in the dark. He wanted to warn her against behaving that way, but Jacqueline had enough experience in this business to know better. And he could not escape the feeling that this whole situation was beyond his control, that Jacqueline was no longer his subordinate and would not be taking direction from him. He asserted his independence in the only way he thought open to him.

"Where do you want to have your talk with the police?" he said.

It was hard to read Jacqueline's expression these days, but Norman thought perhaps she looked a little dismayed.

"Have you called the police?" she said.

"No," said Norman. "They asked me to tell you to call them."

"Good," said Jacqueline. "I'll call them as soon as I get the chance. Now why don't you have Louise schedule your interviews, and I'll have Cheryl schedule mine."

Norman did not particularly like working with Louise, and he realized that scheduling termination interviews might require a degree of subtlety and tact that she lacked. In any case, he didn't want the job handled by a gum chewer. "I'd rather work with Cheryl."

"I've already started the work with Cheryl," said Jacqueline. "Let's not waste the time she's put in so far."

Norman felt he was being squeezed again and was a little surprised at both the anger that welled up in him and what it made him say. "I'm still the manager of this department. I decide how the work will be scheduled. Cheryl is working with me."

If he was surprised at his own little outburst, he was even more surprised at Jacqueline's reaction.

"Yes, sir," she said.

Although it was difficult for Norman to tell with her permanent expression of exhaustion, she didn't seem to be sarcastic.

When she left Norman's office to go to her own, he puzzled over her reaction. Jacqueline had never shown any reverence for authority, particularly his. She certainly had never addressed him as "sir" before. He wondered if working so closely with Pierce was changing her attitude. It had seemed to affect her hygiene, so why not her work style?

Norman called Cheryl into his office and gave her a stack of termination memos.

"I need you to make appointments with these people for me. I will not be doing anything else for the next week. See if you can get the first one in here by this afternoon. After that, just schedule them as you can and give me a list of them once or twice a day. Allow forty-five minutes for each one." It really only takes about fifteen minutes to fire someone, but Norman wanted to make sure the employees wouldn't have any chance of encountering each other in the Human Resources office.

Cheryl looked down at the memos in her hand and nodded.

"This is delicate business, Cheryl," said Norman.

"These people are being terminated as a result of a major reorganization. You should schedule these appointments discreetly, and when the people come here you should be sympathetic. I don't think I have to tell you that everything must be done with the strictest confidentiality."

Cheryl nodded solemnly, and Norman was gratified to see by her expression that he'd made a good choice in her. He sent her back to her desk.

He started up his computer and called up the file of the managers handbook to give himself something to do. He was up to the chapter on overtime policies. He decided to go to the department kitchen and get a cup of coffee before he started writing.

When he walked through the outer office, he saw that Louise was away from her desk, probably getting her orders from Jacqueline. Cheryl was on the telephone.

She lowered her voice as he walked past. He was glad to see her working so efficiently and discreetly. He walked down the hallway to the little kitchen and went in to find his coffee mug, the one with the picture of the timber wolf on it and the phrase "Save the Wildlife" printed below the wolf's portrait. He looked at it for a minute before pouring coffee into it. Save the Wildlife. Doesn't anybody care about the domesticated life?

He poured in dark, acrid coffee, which appeared to have been there on the hot plate for a week. Then he stood for a long time stirring in the off-white powder that they kept there to cut the sharp taste of overcooked coffee. He took the mug and walked slowly back up the little hallway, his footsteps silent on the carpeting. As he neared the doorway to the outer office, he could hear Cheryl on the telephone. There was excitement in her voice, barely restrained by a simulated solemnity.

"Such carnage, Mother. Forty-five people. They put me in charge of scheduling the exit interviews. The last time we had a layoff, a man committed suicide and—"

She stopped talking and looked at Norman gravely when he entered the room. Norman didn't criticize her. He just walked into his office and sat down with his coffee. Cheryl was clearly relishing her role in this process of grinding up forty-five people. Why not? She wasn't responsible for any of it. She could bring these poor people into Norman's abattoir without any pang of conscience. In the Biomethods chain of being, she'd been elevated from the position of human being to angel. She was the angel of retribution.

He sat down in front of his computer and went back to work on his managers handbook. He managed to lose himself in a complicated description of Biomethods' overtime policies and authorization procedures. When he had written three pages on them, he checked his watch and saw that an hour had gone by. He wondered why Cheryl had not yet given him a progress report, but he was just as pleased that nothing had happened yet. He reached for his coffee cup and saw that it was empty.

"Norman?"

Norman put down the coffee cup and swiveled his chair around to face the doorway. Louise was standing there.

"Yes?"

"May I talk to you? Privately?"

Norman did not want to talk to Louise privately, but he believed managers should always grant such requests. He motioned for her to come in.

She closed the door behind her and sat in the chair across from his desk. "I'm worried about Jacqueline."

Norman decided it would be unmanagerial of him to tell her she wasn't the only one. "What do you mean?"

"You must have noticed how strange she's looked." Louise looked scared.

"She does look pretty tired, doesn't she."

"Tired?" Louise was so agitated that her elaborate hair seemed to shake. "Norman, she looks dead."

Norman felt like he had enough problems without adding the sudden onset of staff insanity. "Louise, do you have something serious to tell me?"

"I am serious, Norman. Look how pale she is. She's stopped taking care of herself. She sits in that conference room with all the lights off."

"I know her behavior has been a little—"

"She has a bruise on her neck."

"I don't think—"

"Face it, Norman. Jacqueline is under the control of a vampire. I know the signs."

Norman sat for the next thirty minutes listening to Louise's ravings about vampires, revenants, life force, and a host of things Norman neither believed in nor cared about. She was perfectly calm about her recitation, but the content of it was utterly insane. When she got to the end of her explanation, however, she said something that made all the rest of it seem quite balanced.

"She's going to have to be staked, Norman."

"Staked?" Norman hoped somehow he had misunderstood what she was saying.

"Maybe not right away," said Louise. "I don't think she's completed her transformation yet. But soon."

Norman couldn't really believe she was saying these things. Even Louise usually made more sense than this. "What are you talking about, Louise?"

"It will be the only way to give her release."

"Release from what?"

"She'll be grateful for it, believe me. Oh, she'll fight with all her strength to prevent it, but she'll be grateful for it. They always are."

A part of Norman told him he should throw her out of his office, but the rest of him realized she might be dangerous, and it was up to him to deal with it. He wondered what he should do.

"Don't believe any of that stuff about a special kind of wood," said Louise. "Anything you can drive through the heart will do the job."

"Louise," said Norman. "I'm going to call Security."

"Most people just don't have the fortitude to drive a stake through a body that looks like a human being. Some vampires will make it even harder by changing themselves to look like somebody close to you. Can you imagine how hard it would be to stake a creature that looks like, say, your mother?"

Norman was at a loss as to how to answer, but Louise didn't seem to be looking for a response anyway.

"Once you knock the stake in, the vampire screams, whether they're awake or asleep, it doesn't matter. They might try to grab at you and say things to you to get you to stop. Usually, the second time you hit the stake, they start bleeding from the mouth. This is a sign the force is leaving them. When you hit them again, the vampire's body will get old and withered before your eyes, depending on how old they really are. Sometimes they even turn into dust."

Norman picked up the phone and said again, "I'm going to call Security."

"I'm telling you all this because it's your responsibility, Norman."

Norman started to punch in the extension number for Security, and there was a knock at the door.

Louise looked terrified. She didn't speak but mouthed "Don't answer it."

"Yes?" said Norman.

Jacqueline's voice came from the other side of the door. "Norman, is Louise in there?"

Norman looked at Louise. Her eyes were wide and she began to shake her head.

Norman didn't know what to say.

But Jacqueline saved him the trouble by opening the door. "Oh, there you are, Louise. I've decided to let you take the rest of the day off."

Norman saw there was a Security man standing behind Jacqueline.

Louise seemed to understand the futility of resisting the burly Security man and went quietly, until they got to the outer office. She made a break for her desk and was scrambling to open the drawer when the Security man grabbed her arm and wrenched her away.

"I just need to get my things," she said.

"There's no time for that, Louise," said Jacqueline. "You have an appointment to keep."

"Let her get her things," said Cheryl.

Jacqueline's glance silenced her. Cheryl went to her desk and sat down.

Jacqueline walked with the Security man as far as the outer office doorway. The Security man dragged Louise through the doorway toward the elevator. Louise managed to pull back into the doorway for a moment, and her wide-eyed stare finally settled on Norman.

"Remember what I told you," she said.

The Security man yanked her away.

Norman heard the elevator door rumble shut a moment later. Jacqueline walked back from the doorway to where Norman was standing. "Maybe we could have Cheryl schedule both the hiring interviews and the termination interviews."

"I guess so." Norman, avoiding her eyes, noticed that his shoes needed shining.

"It should work out OK," said Jacqueline, "as long as she doesn't mix them up."

Norman looked up at her and saw she was smiling.

"It was a joke, Norman."

Norman laughed politely.

"At least she had already managed to schedule the day's first interview," sighed Jacqueline. "One candidate was available to meet us on very short notice. She's local, and she said she'd be willing to come right over."

Norman barely heard what she was saying. He was trying to fit everything together in his mind.

The elevator just outside the outer office chimed.

"This is probably our candidate now," said Jacqueline.

Norman heard the elevator door rumble shut. He looked up toward the doorway absently to see whom Jacqueline was talking about. He was surprised to see Gwen walk in.

"Oh, good," said Jacqueline. "It is."

FOURTEEN

PIERCE loved the dirty, noisy, ugly environment of Manchester in 1810. It pulsed with the energy of entrepreneurial success. The people of Manchester believed their mills, with their spinning frames and power looms, were clothing the world, and they believed it with good reason.

Vidalon-le-Haut was long behind him, but Pierce still followed his habit of going to the countryside to feed, although the countryside around Manchester grew ever more sparse with the great shift in manufacturing processes that was taking place.

For his spring feeding in 1810, he chose a weaver's cottage. He entered the cottage several hours before dawn. He found nearly half the living room given over to a loom that sat in a boxlike frame of stout timbers. It was an antique, although it obviously remained in daily use. He examined it. He could see how a treadle below the breast beam would lift the harness to raise the warp yarn and then lower it after the weaver had tripped the lever to shoot the shuttle under it. Another treadle would swing a batten against the woven cloth to tighten it. And another would simultaneously advance the cloth roll on the breast beam and the yarn on the warp beam. It was an ingenious machine.

Pierce had always enjoyed studying machines. He delighted in the way they revealed their nature to one who approached them thoughtfully. This loom clearly illustrated the five steps of weaving: letting off, shedding, picking, beating, and taking up.

He could imagine this weaving family at work: the father sitting at the breast beam, operating the shuttle and the treadles; the youngest son on top of the loom's frame, managing the heddles in their harness; the mother and the rest of the children winding bobbins for the shuttle or cleaning the fluff from the previous day's cloth. It was a pleasant domestic scene, and Pierce knew it was capable of creating five to six yards of plainweave cloth in a day. It was work that strengthened the ties of family but — at five to six yards of cloth a day — contributed little to the task of clothing the world.

This family had several bolts of cloth piled up in the corner of the living room for their merchant. It was dobby, and Pierce judged there was no mill in the vicinity capable of producing this specialty cloth on a power loom, which explained how this family continued to survive. There was enough cloth there that a merchant might be arriving tomorrow.

Across the room from the bolts of cloth, there were three children asleep on a pallet. The parents, and whatever infants the family might have, probably slept in the cottage's only other room. Pierce crept over and picked up a sleeping child. He chose the largest one, as he wanted to leave the smallest for sitting on the loom frame tomorrow. It was a boy, and he remained asleep even as Pierce picked him up. Pierce judged him to be about ten years old. He took him away from the other children and fed lightly on him. The boy never waked.

He took only as much as he needed. Nevertheless, he suspected the child might be too tired to work the next day. He hoped the parents would understand. He put the boy back among the others.

As Pierce left the cottage and stepped back into the cool night air, he reflected on the anachronism of this family. They were one of a handful of families that did putting-out work, and soon there would be none. From the earliest times, home was the logical place to work, and here in the countryside around Manchester, for centuries, weavers had earned their keep from merchants who put the work out to them. The merchant brought a supply of cotton thread and part-wages to the home and then returned to collect the cloth and pay the rest of the wages when the weaving was finished.

In 1764, a man named James Hargreaves invented the spinning jenny, a machine that spun thread from cotton fibers and allowed spinners to produce much more thread than they had ever done by hand. Then in 1769, Richard Arkwright connected this machine to water turbines, and it made so much thread so quickly it began to put the spinners out of work. Pierce had fed on the sons of both Hargreaves and Arkwright shortly after he had arrived here in 1792.

The boom in thread production had meant more weaving and, until quite recently, weavers were among the most prosperous workers. They enjoyed steadily increasing wages until the end of the century.

But Arkwright had taken an irreversible step when he emancipated manufacturing from human power. And in the later years of the century, English engineers and inventors began applying mechanical power to every step of the cloth-making process. By the turn of the century, Manchester was dotted with mills bearing smokestacks, and a lively trade sprang up to supply coal to the mills to burn and make the steam to power spinning machines and looms. Such mills belched out cotton cloth and smoke in equal quantities. They produced cloth so much faster than the weavers in the countryside that wages fell by one third over the first decade of the century.

In 1810, the putting-out system was in the final throes of collapse. Weavers had begun to move their families into Manchester to search for opportunities to make a living. The dirty, noisy, dangerous steam-powered mills were waiting for them when they arrived.

The population of Manchester had grown explosively at the turn of the century. Wages continued to fall, and there were more and more people competing for less and less pay. Even so, most workers earned more money in Manchester's mills than the weavers had earned in their homes. The difference was in the control of the work. Under the putting-out system, workers planned their work and decided when to start, when to quit, how fast to proceed. But in the mills, these were not matters for worker decision; they were controlled by the power looms, which wove at their own breakneck pace without regard to the desires of the operators.

Since Pierce had arrived in this region, thousands of impoverished and exhausted families had come to Manchester, and their numbers increased daily.

Manchester had none of the problems with worker disobedience that Pierce had seen at Vidalon-le-Haut. There were more workers than positions, and the prevailing wage fell every year. Workers struggled more with each other than they did with employers. The feast days and the generous gifts that the Montgolfiers had used to such good effect were nowhere to be found in Manchester.

Living conditions were crowded. Streets and common areas were dirty. Factories were dangerous, and the very air outside was acrid with the taste of burning coal. Pierce thought the city looked like Hell on Earth, but as filthy and dangerous as it was, it was the new age of humanity.

*   *   *

The previous age had died in Paris in 1792. It died with Louis XVI, who embodied much of what was good and most of what was bad about the old regime. Rarely had the world seen a kinder man, or one less competent to guide the energies of a society liberated from respect for its oldest (and most infirm, perhaps) institutions. He went to his death with both dignity and helplessness, and Pierce considered witnessing the event one of his critical life moments.

A thick fog had drifted into Revolution Plaza before dawn that day, damping sound and dampening clothing. A regiment of soldiers entered the plaza with the fog and adopted a square formation around the scaffold, at a distance of 100 feet. Then a detail was sent to clear the area around the scaffold of onlookers.

More people drifted into the plaza, but they were orderly and well behaved. Pierce did not see any of the vendors of refreshments and souvenirs (tricolor cockades, replicas of the guillotine, dolls with separable heads) that were usually present at executions, and at first he thought the soldiers were stopping them outside the plaza. But the crowd seemed so somber that he eventually concluded the vendors had remained at home, or at least had left their wares there, of their own accord.

It was eight o'clock before the first of the 1,200-soldier escort entered the plaza with the King's coach. The plaza guards opened their square formation to admit the coach, which then rolled slowly into the empty area before the scaffold behind a pair of well-mannered horses. The soldiers closed ranks once again, keeping the people at a distance from the man their justice was about to dispatch.

There was some confusion while the escort sorted itself among the crowd of ordinary citizens, and Pierce heard officers barking orders to organize the troops, mounted and foot, in ranks that filled the plaza.

Once the escort was quiet again, a man in a plain, dark coat opened the door of the coach, and the King emerged, climbing down the steps of the coach to the stone pavement. A priest climbed out of the coach after him and stood near him, speaking closely into his ear. The King was a portly man of middling height, and Pierce was surprised at the stature he managed to convey. He stood straight and, perhaps, a little defiant. His wig curled into a pair of rolls on either side of his head, and in back hung down in more curls. Pierce thought him rather gallant in caring enough for his appearance to wear a wig to the scaffold.

There was some commotion in the crowd across the plaza from where Pierce was standing. Horses were prancing and men running about. Pierce could not see what was happening in the thick of the disturbance, but he heard shouts and a single phrase emerged from the hubbub.

". . . save the King!"

But the ranks of soldiers never moved, despite the commotion behind them, and the shouting died away after a moment. Everything became quiet again. The King, with the priest still speaking into his ear, and the dark-coated man following him stepped toward the scaffold.

The executioner and his two assistants met the King at the foot of the steps. One of the assistants grasped the lapel of the King's coat to help him remove it, and the King yanked it back away from the man. In the midst of the conflict, the priest was unable to keep his place at the King's ear and stepped back for a moment.

Pierce was not close enough to hear any conversation, but he could see the King take hold of the laps of his coat as if refusing to part with it. The executioner and his assistants stood uncertainly for a moment, then began to move toward the King resolutely. The dark-coated man held up a hand to stop them and had a short conversation with the King.

The King finally nodded. The dark-coated man gestured to the executioner. The King then stood with his chin up as one of the executioner's assistants removed his coat. The King managed to make the man appear to be his valet rather than one of the instruments of his death. The other assistant tied the King's wrists behind his back, and still Louis looked more like he was the director than the victim of the affair. The priest stepped in close again to resume speaking in his ear.

Pierce wondered if the King was as annoyed as he himself would be with a priest speaking in his ear that way.

When the King began to ascend the steps to the platform with his hands tied, he almost slipped. The priest, still speaking steadily, supported the King as he climbed the steep steps to the platform six feet above.

The executioner followed him up to the platform.

The King stood in the damp, chilly fog, coatless, his hands tied behind him, and turned to face the crowd. The priest stepped back away from him. The executioner approached him with a large pair of shears. For a moment, Pierce thought perhaps the executioner was attempting a whole new style of execution, until he saw the executioner grasp the hair that flowed down the King's back and use the shears to remove a great hank of it in three competent snips. So it had not been a wig, after all.

The King, his neck bare at the back, then nodded at the executioner, with a great deal of dignity Pierce thought, and began to address the crowd.

"I die innocent of all the crimes—" he began.

But the executioner made a hand signal, and a drum roll was started from among the ranks of the soldiers. The drums continued while the executioner grabbed the King, who attempted to speak over the drums, and pushed him down on the plank. The King did not struggle, and the executioner strapped him down efficiently, then slid the plank into position. Even strapped to the plank like a roll of carpet, the King appeared dignified.

With the drums still rolling, the executioner pushed the plank home, thrusting the King's head into the brace. He then grasped the trip cord of the guillotine and pulled it. The swish of the twelve-inch blade as it plummeted in

its tracks could not be heard over the drums. The drum-
mers were so masterful that they ended the roll with a
single loud thump at the exact instant the blade hit home.
And that loud thump was followed by the second, quieter
thump of the King's head in the basket in front of the
guillotine.

When the King's head left his body, his neck
expressed a jet of blood to a distance of nearly three feet,
but the pressure gave out with the expiration of his stout
heart, and the executioner was able to reach into the
basket immediately and pull out the severed head by the
hair without peril of being soaked. He held the head, drip-
ping, before him and turned slowly about on the platform
to let most of the crowd get a view of their late King's
face: prominent nose, pudgy cheeks, closed eyes, relaxed
mouth. The people in the crowd stared at the face as if
searching it for some sign of forgiveness or clemency.

Blood continued to run from the King's headless body,
out of the stump of the neck and down on to the platform,
but Pierce thought there was less of it than one might
expect.

No one spoke that Pierce could hear.

Finally, an officer barked an order, and the soldiers
began to reform themselves to depart the plaza. The
executioner dropped the King's head back into the basket
without ceremony and took a bandana from his pocket to
wipe his hands. He then descended by the stairs as the
soldiers were leaving.

The crowd stood silently.

Pierce watched the blood drip slowly from the stump
of the King's neck. Louis XVI was the embodiment of an
age, and now that age lay headless and bleeding on the
platform of a guillotine.

The people of France wanted a new way of life, and
they thought the only way to get it was to raze the old
way. They were right, of course, but few of them under-

stood how many executions would have to take place before the razing was accomplished.

He looked around at the people who stood there so quietly. There were aristocrats in waistcoats and silk knee breeches, penny-earners in rags, fine ladies with elaborate hair arrangements . . . sans culottes, washer women, shop keepers, lawyers, soldiers, priests. Pierce wondered how many of them would have to be decapitated before the razing was finished.

He imagined the hundreds, perhaps thousands, of heads that would drop into the basket up on that scaffold before this change was complete, and it sickened him.

FIFTEEN

"WHERE'S Mommy?" said Megan.

"She's at the office. I imagine she'll be a little late this evening." Norman opened the dishwasher. A puff of vapor escaped, and he reached in to pull out a handful of silverware. It was still warm from being washed. He handed it to his daughter. "Start setting the table, please."

Megan went into the dining room, and Norman continued unloading the dishwasher. He took three or four dishes out at a time and jostled them into a stack as he walked to the other side of the kitchen to put them away. He was still doing this when Megan came back into the kitchen.

"Daddy, why are you putting the dishes in the trash?"

Norman looked and saw that he was standing in front of the trash can. There were a half dozen dinner plates piled in among the used paper towels and banana skins. He took them back out and carried them over to the sink. "I was thinking about something else," he said.

"I'll finish it for you," said Megan. "Go watch television with Justin."

"Good idea." Norman tried to hide his chagrin at taking direction from a ten-year-old girl, but she did seem to have control of the situation. Why did everybody seem to be in control but him? He looked around for his scotch bottle. Then he remembered he'd already finished it. He started toward the living room heavily.

"Daddy?"

He stopped and turned back toward Megan.

"Should I set a place for Mommy tonight?"

"I don't know," said Norman. "I wasn't able to ask her if she'd be home for dinner."

Norman needed to talk with someone. He needed to whine about the feelings of betrayal and dismay he'd felt when his wife arrived at his company for a job interview. He needed to moan that he hated his job, but it was the only job he had. He needed to blubber that his boss and his subordinate had formed a relationship and that he felt trapped by it. He needed to tell someone how hard it had been to fire the assistant manager of corporate communications that afternoon. He needed to describe how the man had cried and how Norman had not been able to do any more than offer him a kleenex from a box on his desk.

He wondered when Gwen would get home. The last time he'd seen her was at the office, as Jacqueline escorted her upstairs. Norman had been able to wave to her, but that was all. Jacqueline took her all around the company to see the entire operation, although she had apparently skipped Norman and briefed her on Human Resources herself. He hadn't seen her again before he had to leave for home, so he just left without talking to her.

Norman sat in front of the television with Justin without perceiving any of the broadcast. His mind kept drifting back to company policy. Biomethods did not hire relatives of employees. The company could not both hire Gwen and keep Norman. Norman was realistic enough to know which choice the company was likely to take. It was likely to let Norman go. In Pierce's strange vocabulary, it would be "kinder" that way.

The rest of the evening — watching television with Justin, making dinner, eating with the kids — was a fog. Norman went through the motions, grateful that he was capable of doing the work in a state of preoccupation and grateful the kids were there to keep him from doing things like putting dishes in the trash. He decided that when Gwen got home, he was going to have it out with her. He had always felt he would give her anything or do anything for her, but that was when he thought she would never ask him to. When he thought of her meeting other people in the company, joking pleasantly and comporting herself like a high-powered executive, he wondered what they must think of him. This is Norman's wife? Can you believe this high-powered woman is married to *Norman*?

He had gotten the kids into bed and was standing in the living room, trying to decide whether to go out to the store for a bottle of scotch, when he heard the sound of the kitchen door opening and closing, followed by the metallic splatter of a set of keys on the kitchen table. Gwen appeared in the doorway.

She was pale and haggard, like she'd been in job interviews all day, only worse maybe.

"Did you get any dinner?" he said.

She made a face. "I'm not hungry. My stomach's upset."

They stood looking at each other for a moment, and Norman once again had that feeling that he didn't really know her.

"Are the kids in bed?" she said.

"Yeah." Norman couldn't come up with the right words for starting a confrontation.

"Are you upset, Norman?"

"Of course not," said Norman. "Why should I be upset? A stranger comes into my company and takes away the only part of my job that makes me feel decent. Then my wife goes behind my back to undermine my position in the firm. Why should any of that upset me?"

"I'm not undermining your position." Gwen tossed her portfolio on the sofa about as gently as she had handled Norman's ego.

Norman noticed for the first time how awful she looked. She wasn't just pale. She was kind of drawn-looking. She looked nearly as tired as Jacqueline. "Are you all right?"

"He wants a lot in return when he gives you a job."

"Did he harass you sexually?" said Norman.

"I wouldn't call it that," said Gwen. "I don't find it very easy to talk about. I don't feel well. I think I'll go to bed now." She did not start toward the bedroom right away, but seemed to wait for herself to follow her orders, as if she were dealing with a resistant subordinate.

Norman looked at her stupidly. He was the one who wasn't feeling well. How could she not be feeling well, too? The two of them stood there in silence, and Norman felt betrayed, confused, humiliated, and scared all at once. It crossed his mind that this state really was normal. Much of humanity probably felt this way much of the time. The doorbell rang.

Gwen continued staring at the wall and didn't even seem to hear it. Norman studied her, wondering what was wrong.

The doorbell rang again.

Norman went to the door. When he opened it, he found Cheryl standing on the front step under the light.

"Cheryl, what are you doing here?"

"They got Louise." She pushed past him into the living room.

Norman followed her into his living room. "What are you doing here?"

She stopped in the living room and stood facing Gwen. "I'm too late."

"Cheryl," Norman said as he came up beside her, "why are you at my house?"

"Louise told me what was going on before they took her away." Cheryl turned to Norman. "I didn't believe it. But this evening I went to see her, and she's missing. Her family hasn't seen her.

"All this time," said Cheryl, "I thought it was simply

the ravings of an undereducated, superstitious mind. But
Louise was right. There are more things in this world than
you can learn about in college. There are vampires loose in
the company, Norman. They got that technician in the
Arthritis Department. They got Louise, and now it looks
like they're getting your wife."

"What are you talking about?" said Norman.

"Look at her, Norman."

Norman turned to look at Gwen in spite of himself.
She stood before him with her eyes open but apparently
unseeing.

"She's very tired," he said. "Who can I call for you,
Cheryl?"

"Tired, hell." Cheryl walked up close to Gwen and
examined her as if she were a museum exhibit. "She's been
bitten, Norman."

Gwen didn't seem to hear any of this, but stood and
looked off into space.

Between the need to get Cheryl out of his house and
the need to attend to his wife's condition — whatever it
was — Norman found himself unable to establish any
priorities. Why did everything these days seem to turn into
a decision he did not feel competent to make?

"She'll be OK if you can keep her away from them,"
said Cheryl. "But if you try, they'll come looking for her."

"Cheryl, I think you had better go." Norman put his
hand on Gwen's shoulder to direct her toward the bedroom,
and he realized he was trying to pursue two goals at once.

"No," said Cheryl. "I think you had better wake up
and see what's going on."

But Gwen didn't move when he gently began to push
her, and Cheryl showed no sign of leaving. It never works
to try to manage things without priorities. Norman looked
at Gwen and decided she wasn't going anywhere, so he
turned to Cheryl.

"It's time for you to leave, Cheryl. If you don't go now, I'll call the police."

"Don't bother, Norman. The police don't know how to deal with something like this."

"No," said Norman. "I mean I'm going to call them to come and take you away."

"Don't do that, Norman. I'm the only friend you've got."

Norman went into the kitchen and grabbed the phone. He started to dial 911, but he realized he hadn't any idea how he would explain this. He didn't like having Cheryl in his house, but she didn't seem particularly dangerous, either. He heard his front door slam.

He hung up the phone and went back to the living room. When he got there, Cheryl was gone, but so was Gwen.

"Gwen?"

For a helpless moment Norman thought Cheryl had kidnapped Gwen.

He walked down the hallway and into the darkened bedroom. He snapped on the light and found Gwen fully clothed but unconscious on the bed. He went to her and put his hand on her forehead. It felt cold. Alarmed, he checked her pulse. It seemed slow and irregular.

"Gwen?"

She was perfectly still.

In a panic, Norman grabbed the telephone next to the bed and dialed 911 to get an ambulance. He explained to the man who answered the phone that his wife seemed to have gone into a coma. The man asked for Norman's name and address and told him to be out in front of the house to direct the ambulance.

Norman sat on the bed and held Gwen's cool hand. Seconds passed like months, and after about fifty years he heard a siren in the distance. He got up to go out in front of the house as he'd been told to do.

Out in his front yard, he could see the flashing lights of the ambulance, but the siren had stopped. Norman stood in the front yard and waved. The ambulance stopped right in front of the house, and two uniformed men bounded from the doors. They ran around to the rear door to take a wheeled stretcher out. Norman led them in through the front door and to the bedroom. The bed was empty.

"She's not there," said Norman.

"Where's the bathroom?" said one of the paramedics.

Norman pointed toward the bathroom off the master bedroom. The paramedic went in, then came out shaking his head. Norman noticed the bedroom window was open, but he didn't think Gwen would have left through the window. It just didn't seem like the kind of thing she would do.

Norman took the paramedics from room to room looking for Gwen. Megan's room was dark, and she called out when the shaft of light laid across her on her bed.

"It's OK, Meg." Norman looked around the room, but there was no sign of Gwen. "Go back to sleep."

In Justin's room, they found the lights on and Justin asleep, sitting on the side of his bed in his pajamas. Norman went over, laid him down, and pulled the bedclothes over him before he went back out into the hallway with the paramedics and shut the door.

"I don't understand," said Norman.

"They're going to have to bill you for this anyway," said one of the paramedics. "It's counted as a call as soon as we leave the garage."

"Yeah. Fine." Norman didn't care about the bill. He just wanted to find Gwen.

But the paramedics apparently had other work to do.

Norman followed them to the door. He stood on his doorstep looking up and down the street while the paramedics packed up their wheeled stretcher and left. They drove off quietly, but with their red-and-white lights blinking. As the ambulance glided down the street, its emergency lights swept over a human figure on the sidewalk.

Norman sprinted up the block toward the figure, but as he neared it he realized it was moving toward his house and not away from it. And it didn't have Gwen's walk anyway. He stopped and waited under a streetlight for it.

When the figure came into the light, Norman saw that it was Cheryl. She was carrying something. She walked up to him and put into his hands a croquet mallet and a stake with colored stripes.

"You might need these."

"Did you see anybody on this street?" said Norman.

"She took off, huh."

"I don't know." Norman gestured helplessly with the mallet. "But she's gone."

"You can find her at the office," said Cheryl.

Norman didn't believe her, but she behaved and spoke with such confidence that he began to doubt himself. Her behavior reminded him of the way she managed the company's group insurance plans: an extraordinary grasp of the details combined with an inflexible sense of the way things should work.

"They're probably just starting work over there," she said. "She's been called by her master.

"Get a grip on yourself, Norman. Let's go back in the house. I'm going to explain to you what's going on and what you have to do."

Sixteen

Britain in general and Manchester in particular still smarted from the Slater affair. Samuel Slater, an apprentice in Mr. Arkwright's spinning mill, emigrated to America in 1789 under the sponsorship of a merchant from Providence, Rhode Island. Textile mill apprentices were available in great quantity, and no one mourned his loss for the British textile industry — until he began building America's first spinning mill. Soon, Providence, Rhode Island was producing as much cotton thread as the American weavers could use.

The British were outraged that the loss of an apprentice could improve the competitive position of a trading partner. The United States, to the British way of thinking, was supposed to *buy* cotton thread, not make it. Parliament passed one law forbidding the emigration of textile workers and another forbidding the export of textile manufacturing machinery or parts. Mill owners understood it was their national duty to protect their manufacturing processes and keep them secret. The spinning jenny may have escaped, and the knowledge of mechanical carding was already widespread, but the government was determined Britain would own an international monopoly on the power loom.

Pierce decided he should be the one to bring the power loom to America. He was certain it would mean a fortune, but that was not what tempted him. He looked around squalid Manchester and saw what a dirty, dangerous, unhealthy place it was, and he was inspired by the challenge of determining if textile manufacturing could be done in a way that was healthy for the people engaged in it. There was no way to find out unless he had a power loom.

Pierce picked out the Little Company mill, which was named not for its size but for its founder, Mr. Asa Little. He chose the Little Company because it was neither the largest nor the smallest of Manchester's weaving mills. The smallest of them lacked the more modern machinery, and the largest of them were too well watched by both their owners and the customs officers.

With the limitless patience of which he was capable, Pierce watched the mill for a week. He stood outside the mill gate on his first day and saw the furnace crew arrive two hours before dawn. There were five of them, and a watchman admitted them and then locked the gate after them. They arrived early, Pierce suspected, to stoke the fire for the mill's boiler. The sounds of their work carried to him across the mill yard, and in the quiet of the morning he heard them talking and laughing over the crashes of their shovels into the coal piles. It was a full moon, and he watched the wispy exhaust of the overnight fire grow into a great dark pillar of viscous smoke pouring out of the smokestack.

The interior of the mill began to give out a chuffing sound, and Pierce judged the mill's great engine had begun to turn. The engine would drive a large vertical shaft that ran up the center of the four-story building. The shaft bore a crown gear at each story, and it spun at a prodigious rate all day long. Each floor of the building then had smaller shafts running perpendicular to the central shaft, with crown gears that could be engaged to the larger one. When they were, these shafts would spin, powering pulleys at regular intervals. A leather belt could convey the spinning energy of the shaft to a pulley or roller driving a power loom.

A piercing whistle sounded from the mill's engine, and

within minutes people began to arrive and line up at the
gate. There were only a handful at first, but ten minutes
later another whistle sounded and they began to arrive in
larger numbers — men, women, and children of all ages,
singly and in groups. Each carried a bundle or a bucket of
some sort, and Pierce judged that it was food. They silently
queued up at the gate. It was morning, but their expres-
sions and posture suggested exhaustion. They reminded
Pierce of something, and it took him a moment to realize
that they all looked the way people normally looked after
he'd fed on them.

At the sound of the third whistle, the watchman
unlocked the gate and a hundred or so people began to
quickly file through. They hastened themselves, more out of
fear than eagerness, Pierce judged. A well-fed man in a
dark suit arrived while they were filing through the gate.
He spoke to no one, and no one spoke to him.

In ten minutes, everyone was through the gate. The
well-fed man gestured to the watchman, who closed the
gate and locked it. Pierce heard the grinding and clacking
of the looms as the operators engaged their machines to
the power shaft. The workday had begun. He consulted his
pocket watch. It was five o'clock.

Pierce watched the mill as the sun arrived over the
horizon. It appeared like a dirty bronze disc in the haze of
the smoke created by the mill and others like it all over
Manchester. Even as the sun climbed upward, the sky
remained as dark as dusk. The chuffing, clacking, and roar-
ing sounds continued unabated, and the column from the
smokestack was so thick and impenetrable it appeared
solid.

Pierce watched the routine for seven days. It never
varied until Sunday, when the mill remained idle the
entire day, except for two men whom he saw between the
mill building and the fence from time to time. He judged

they were there to guard and to make sure the furnace's smoldering fire did not go out completely.

The following week, Pierce called on Mr. Little at his mill. He came to the mill gate and said he wished to purchase cloth. The watchman nodded, admitted him, and gestured toward a door in the mill building off to one side of the door through which Pierce had seen the workers enter. Pierce went in this door and stated his business to a clerk who, writing at a high desk, looked rather like a stork. The clerk climbed down from his stool and went into another room. The floor vibrated slightly and the roar of the machinery, although muted, was ever present.

After a few moments, the clerk returned and ushered Pierce into the other room.

Mr. Little was the well-fed man Pierce had seen supervising the locking of the mill gate each morning. He sat behind a large desk piled with a dozen ledger books and three canoe-shaped wooden objects Pierce recognized as loom shuttles.

"Mr. Pierce." Little stood from his desk. "My secretary says you are interested in purchasing some cloth."

Pierce had been studying textiles for a month and was prepared with his answer. "I wish to supply a dry goods merchant in New England. He needs 3,000 yards of fancy goods, finely woven but durable. If the Little Company can produce the cloth to his specifications, he expects to repeat the order seasonally."

Mr. Little's eyes seemed to light up at the prospect of a standing order. "What are the specifications?"

"Heavy sheeting of number fourteen yarn," said Pierce. "Thirty-seven inches wide, forty-four picks to the inch, and weighing something less than a pound for three yards."

"We mill such cloth regularly," said Mr. Little.

"As you can well imagine," said Pierce, "it is not read-ily available in America. What is the rate for such fancy goods?"

Mr. Little took a pencil from his drawer and opened one of his ledgers to the back pages. He began writing in the book. After a moment, he looked up. "Our basic charge for that quantity of such cloth is 208 pounds, one half down and one half on delivery."

Pierce never expected to take delivery on the cloth, but 104 pounds was not too much to pay for a power loom. He took a roll of banknotes from his purse and began counting them out. "Here is the down payment. Have you a standard contract for a sale such as this?"

Mr. Little's eyes were still glittering when he looked at the pile of banknotes. "I have no need of a contract for a gentleman such as yourself," he said. "Your handshake is as much as I need." He extended his hand.

Pierce had no choice but to shake his hand. When he grasped it, the man looked as if Pierce had handed him a fish. But he did not let Pierce's skin temperature preoccupy him and instead attended to the pile of banknotes, organizing them into a small stack. "Most people would manage such a transaction with a letter of credit."

"I find cash is less expensive," said Pierce.

Mr. Little consulted his pocket watch. "May I offer you some tea, Mr. Pierce?"

Pierce did not ordinarily drink, but he had learned to simulate it, and he agreed as a way of strengthening his friendship with the man.

Mr. Little called to his secretary and asked for tea.

Pierce gestured at the shuttles on the desk. "Are these objects loom shuttles, Mr. Little?"

"Why, yes." Mr. Little held one up. "You see, the bobbin fits in the cavity here, and the thread unwinds freely through this opening when it shoots through the shed of the warp yarn."

"Why is it pointed at each end?" said Pierce.

"The shuttle, of course, travels in either direction. I believe the ends are tapered to allow it a more accurate passage in its journey across the loom. It moves quite rapidly, you know."

The secretary, a young man wearing spectacles, brought an indifferent-looking teapot and two stout cups on a tray.

The two men chatted amiably while Mr. Little slurped from his cup noisily and Pierce pretended to sip from his. Pierce asked the mill owner about the manufacturing process and the machines that accomplished it.

"Are you English, Mr. Pierce?"

"No."

"I thought not." Mr. Little slurped more tea, then put the cup down. "I am forbidden by law to let you have a power loom or any part of one or any designs, plans, or diagrams. But there is no law against discussing it."

Pierce pretended to take another sip of tea.

"We in the British textile industry have a sacred national trust. We must protect our manufacturing techniques in order to maintain Britain's industrial hegemony. But you and I can talk as much as we want. I might even show you the machines in operation. Without the parts to make one, the knowledge of a power loom's operations is useless to anyone who wishes to profit by it. It's not as if you could memorize the shape of each of its three hundred and eighty-seven parts, is it?"

Mr. Little evidently thought this a marvelous joke, and he began to laugh heartily.

"Might I see the machines working, then?" said Pierce.

Mr. Little responded enthusiastically and virtually whisked Pierce out of the office and into the first-floor weave room, where workers tended a dozen power looms.

The noise of the weave room was deafening. Each of the five steps in weaving is a motion, and in a power loom each motion has its own distinctive noise: the drone of the weft yarn against the warp, the hiss of the shuttle along its track, the rhythmic thumping of the leather power belts, the ring of the drive chains. All these sounds combined to create a cacophony that was almost musical.

Overlaying it all was the hum of the great spinning shaft at the center of the building. Pierce could see it in the center of the room, and he noted how its crown gear engaged the smaller drive shafts that ran along the ceiling, with a pulley at each loom station. The great central shaft rotated almost lazily compared to the smaller shafts along the ceiling, and the pulleys at each power loom spun so rapidly that their edges appeared to blur.

Each power loom was attended by two people, and it appeared to be the rule that the team would consist of an adult and a child. Pierce judged a child's small fingers would be useful in some of the manipulations of the weaving process. There was a thin, pinched-looking man in a dark coat who walked up and down the aisle between the rows of power looms, and he appeared to have a knout at his belt.

The man saw Pierce and Mr. Little and came to them directly.

"Mr. Pierce," Mr. Little shouted over the roar of the machinery, "this is our foreman, Stryker."

Stryker bowed, and Pierce bowed in return.

Mr. Little pointed toward one of the looms. "Stryker, why is that machine idle over there?"

"The shuttle has been skipping its track," shouted Stryker. "We are trying to determine the cause."

Pierce could see a man and a child examining the idle machine, which had a quarter roll of dark blue cloth wound on its take-up roll below the breast beam. From time to time, the child glanced nervously in their direction, and Pierce wondered if this surveillance had anything to do with a large, fresh bruise on the side of his face.

"Shuttles skip all the time, Stryker," shouted Mr. Little. "That machine should have half a roll by this time of day."

"We will have it running directly," said Stryker.

"Have it running now," said Mr. Little.

Stryker nodded and walked over to speak with the man at the loom. The child moved to the side of the machine as he approached, as if to put the loom between himself and the foreman.

Pierce could not hear their conversation over the din of the machinery, but it was clear that Stryker instructed the man to engage the loom to the drive shaft. The child watched them from beside the machine. The man shook his head and said something, whereupon Stryker reached for the knout at his belt. The man then turned hastily and threw the tall lever that engaged the machine. It immediately began weaving furiously, heddles lifting the warp yarn, the shuttle shooting first one way and then the other, the rolls winding and unwinding.

Mr. Little leaned over to Pierce and shouted confidentially, "One simply needs to get their attention." He laughed.

As Pierce watched, the wooden shuttle skipped out of its track and shot out of the machine altogether. The child, who was still standing beside the machine, caught it in the shoulder. He fell to the floor. The man immediately disengaged the loom from the drive shaft and went to the child. As other operators around the room saw what had happened, they took their machines off-line and approached the child's crumpled body.

Soon all the machines were idle and most of the workers were clustered around the form of the child on the floor. The room became much quieter, although the hum of the drive shafts was still apparent. Pierce knew the shuttle had come off the machine with the force of a bullet, and he suspected the child's shoulder was shattered.

"What's going on here?" shouted Mr. Little to the room at large. "Stryker, get those machines running."

"This boy seems to be hurt," said Stryker.

"Well then, get him out of here and get the machines running," said Mr. Little.

Stryker nodded and began to disperse the knot of employees, sending them back to their machines.

As the clacking, grinding, and humming started up again, Mr. Little turned to Pierce. "It takes a deal of time to train a foreman," he shouted. "Stryker ought to know by now that we can replace that child easily. There are several of them out by the mill gate right now."

With that, Mr. Little strode off toward a loom that was now operating again on the other side of the room. Pierce followed.

The loom was anchored to the wooden floor and it was engaged to the drive shaft at the ceiling via a leather belt which transferred the spin of a pulley mounted in the drive shaft to a pulley mounted on the end of a shaft in the loom. The shaft in the loom was in center of a great reel of warp yarn located just below the warp beam, and it fed yarn over this beam, which supplied some tension to it, and into a harness that contained the heddles. The machine raised the warp yarn and shot the shuttle under it with a speed that was demonic and a purposefulness that seemed sentient.

Pierce had the feeling that if he stood there long enough, the power loom might speak to him. But it didn't need to. To one who understood weaving, the machine told its story with more clarity than anyone could ever bring to a description of it.

Pierce had studied weaving to prepare himself for this moment, and he knew exactly where all the difficulties in the process would occur. To these areas he gave his greatest attention, estimating the dimensions and memorizing the shapes of the parts connected with them.

While Mr. Little held forth on the cost of the machine, the length of time he'd had to wait to take delivery, and the circumstances of its installation, Pierce walked around it and studied its every nuance and motion. He was careful, however, not to walk past either end of the shuttle track, after seeing what had happened to the child.

Before Mr. Little had finished the story of his acquisition of the machine, which was — admittedly — something of an epic, Pierce understood the mechanism in its entirety. He thanked Mr. Little, set a date to retrieve the cloth he had ordered, and took his leave.

Pierce had no intention of retrieving the cloth. He wanted to leave so he could find paper and pencil and draw a set of plans for the machine, to see if he'd got it right. He would then destroy these plans so as not to be caught with them in his bags at the customs office. But he knew if he could draw them without assistance, it meant he understood the power loom well enough to recreate it in America. He felt rather like Prometheus.

There were three children playing by the mill gate when he left. He paid no attention to them, and he did not turn around when he heard Stryker call to one of them.

Seventeen

WHEN Norman walked in the front door with Cheryl, both kids were waiting in the living room. They stood side by side in the doorway to the corridor that led back to the bedrooms.

"Isn't Mommy home yet?" said Justin.

"No," said Norman. "She's working late again."

Justin shrugged, satisfied, and shuffled back into the corridor.

"I'll come tuck you in shortly," said Norman.

Justin didn't answer. Norman wondered if he was even awake.

"Daddy," said Megan, "what are you doing with a croquet mallet?"

Norman looked down at the mallet in his hands. Cheryl had given him one with green stripes. "Nothing." He gestured at Cheryl, who was still standing beside him. "It belongs to Cheryl. I'm just holding it for her."

"Nobody sells wooden baseball bats anymore," said Cheryl. "Can you believe that? I went to three different sporting goods stores. All the baseball bats are aluminum now."

Megan looked at her. "Who are you?"

"My name's Cheryl, dear. I work for your daddy." Cheryl walked up to Megan and started to hug her.

Megan backed away.

"Good," said Cheryl. "Be careful of strangers. That's good."

"Megan, why don't you go back to bed?" said Norman.

"I'll tell Mommy to come in and say good-night when she gets home."

Megan looked as if she didn't want to go back to bed but considered it the lesser of evils compared to staying in the same room with Cheryl, who obviously aroused her suspicions. "Good night, Daddy." She turned to go.

"Good night, dear," said Cheryl.

Megan glanced sidelong at Cheryl. "Good night."

When Megan was gone, Norman tossed the croquet mallet and the stake on the sofa next to Gwen's portfolio. He thought Cheryl was probably correct that Gwen was at the office, but he wondered why she hadn't taken her portfolio.

"I'll watch the kids so you can go to the office and stake Pierce," said Cheryl.

Norman wasn't going to stake Pierce, but he thought he should take advantage of her offer so he could look for Gwen. "Thanks, Cheryl," he said.

He decided he should put on a clean shirt and necktie if he was going to the office, and he walked back toward the bedroom. He had unbuttoned three buttons of his shirt by the time he reached the bedroom, but as he grabbed the front of the shirt to start pulling it out from his pants, he realized he was behaving as crazily as Cheryl. Was he going to run off and leave his kids in the care of this lunatic?

He turned around and walked slowly back into the living room.

Cheryl was standing next to the coffee table. "What's the matter, Norman?"

"I'm not going, Cheryl," he said.

"Yes, you're right," said Cheryl. "It's too dangerous to do it in the dark. Wait until morning."

"I'm not going to stake him in the morning, either," said Norman. "I'm not going to stake him at all."

"You have to, Norman. He's got your woman."

"Listen to me," said Norman. "You need help."

"Anybody else who had been through everything you've been through would have gotten the message by now, Norman."

"You've lost touch with reality, Cheryl."

"Wake up and smell the corpses," said Cheryl.

"There's only one corpse, Cheryl," said Norman. "Except for Blankenship, of course. But that was before Pierce. I think you should go home now." He reached across the sofa and grabbed the croquet mallet and the stake to hand to her.

Cheryl sighed heavily. "I can't help you if you won't let me."

"I don't want you to help me," said Norman. "I just want you to go."

Cheryl looked thoughtfully at his chest where his shirt was still open, and it crossed Norman's mind that this could all be some sort of ruse for the sake of a sexual encounter. But then he didn't think women usually pursued sex so deviously.

"I'll go, Norman, if you'll answer a couple questions, then listen to what I have to tell you."

Norman thought about it for a moment.

"It can't hurt you," said Cheryl. "Your mind is completely closed. What can you lose?"

"I don't have time for this," said Norman. "My wife is missing. I have to call the police." He dropped the croquet mallet and stake back on the sofa.

"You have enough time to listen to what I have to say," said Cheryl.

Norman didn't want to hear a lot of paranormal clap-trap, but it did seem to be the only way he was going to get rid of her. He sat down heavily on the sofa. "OK."

Cheryl sat down on the sofa beside him.

"I notice you wear a cross, Norman."

Norman put his hand to his chest. Cheryl had seen Blankenship's cross. He felt embarrassed.

"I didn't know you were a religious person," said Cheryl. "I think maybe that's what's protecting you. But your wife doesn't wear a cross, does she?"

"This is all getting rather personal, Cheryl." Norman shifted uncomfortably.

Cheryl reached inside her blouse and pulled out a chain with a cross on it. It looked like a country western version of the one Norman wore. It was gold, decoratively chased, with several gems embedded in it.

"It belonged to Louise." The tears welled up in Cheryl's eyes, and Norman could see some clear liquid forming at the edge of her left nostril. "It's what she was after in her desk drawer. I went through the drawer after they took her away, and I found it." She looked at it, and a tear rolled down her right cheek. "It's not exactly what I might have chosen, but it works. My God, I miss her, Norman. She was right all along, and I ridiculed her for it." Cheryl sniffed, then wiped her nose on her shirt cuff.

Norman had never seen a woman wipe her nose on her shirt cuff before. He got up and went to the kitchen, where he had a box of tissues. He brought it back out to the living room and handed it to Cheryl.

She wiped her nose, balled up the tissue on the coffee table, and took another one. She wiped her face, then blew her nose.

"You've been meeting with the big one all along." Cheryl was more composed when she was talking business. "But he hasn't gone after you yet because of the cross. They can sense when there are holy symbols or relics nearby. He might not have seen your cross yet, but he can sense it."

"You mean Pierce?"

"It all adds up, Norman. Look how suddenly he appeared. He doesn't like to work in the daylight. Ever since meeting alone with him, Jacqueline has looked like death warmed over. Now that technician is dead — bled to death from puncture wounds in the neck. And there's other stuff, too."

"What other stuff?"

"I talk with the admins in other departments, and I've heard things," said Cheryl. "All over the company there are people working strange hours, like Jacqueline. They keep their offices dark, don't change their clothes much. It's all over the company, Norman. It's like a disease."

"Even if it's what you say it is, what do they want with us?"

"That's what I haven't been able to figure out," said Cheryl. "I'm not surprised they would take over a biotechnology company, but it knocked me for a loop when they shut down the AIDS project. You would think they would want the AIDS cure. I imagine AIDS would be no fun for vampires."

"Pierce says there never will be a cure for AIDS." Norman was surprised to hear himself participating, as if this were a serious conversation or something.

"Maybe it doesn't bother them," said Cheryl. "Maybe it just tastes bad, and they have other priorities."

The doorbell rang.

Norman felt a surge of hope, but then he realized Gwen would not have used the bell. He got up and began buttoning his shirt up again.

Cheryl gathered up the mallet and the stake and headed toward the kitchen. "Maybe I'll have to take care of this myself," she said.

Norman realized he didn't want her going out and attacking someone with a mallet and stake. "Wait a minute, Cheryl. Stay."

"I don't get you, Norman," she said.

The doorbell rang again.

"Look," said Norman, "I have to answer the door. Just wait in the kitchen, OK?"

Cheryl shrugged and went into the kitchen.

Norman went to the door and pulled it open. Pierce was standing on his doorstep.

"What are you doing here?" said Norman.

"Hello, Norman." Pierce stood easily on the step under the glare of the outside light. "I just stopped by to make sure Gwen got home all right. She refused a ride, but she looked very tired."

"She *was* tired," said Norman. "She passed out or something."

"Oh?" said Pierce. "Well, I don't think you should worry about her. I'm sure she'll be all right."

"I *am* worried about her," said Norman. "She's missing. I left her in the bedroom, and when I came back she was gone."

Pierce looked uncertain. Norman had never seen him look that way and found it very strange. But he didn't get to study the look, for it passed quickly. Then Pierce muttered one word, turned, and ran into the night.

It was a word that made Norman think perhaps the world was no longer the place he thought it was.

"Jacqueline."

* * *

The parking lot at Biomethods was well lit for security reasons, but there weren't very many cars in it when Norman arrived. He sat in his car and looked at the darkened building for a moment. He said a silent prayer that Justin and Megan would be safe with Cheryl, then he took the croquet mallet and the stake from the seat beside him and climbed out of the car.

There was a part of him that said he should feel silly entering the building in the middle of the night with a croquet mallet. But a larger part of him said the world had become a very strange place and he should be prepared for anything. He looked down at the implements in his hands. The stake was pretty ridiculous, but the mallet would probably come in handy. It had a good, stout head and a long handle. One could grasp the handle with both hands and swing it like a sledge hammer. A two-handed blow with this mallet could crush a skull.

Norman stopped and stood in the parking lot for a moment looking at the front of the office building. Why was he thinking about crushing skulls? He was not the skull-crushing type. Whose skull did he expect to crush anyway?

There was no security guard in the lobby, but the front door was unlocked. It was as if company management had no reason to fear intruders — or maybe invited them. Norman put the stake in his belt and shifted the mallet to his left hand so he could pull the door open with his right. He stepped inside.

Norman did not know what he expected to find. He felt certain that he would not find Pierce, for although his boss had had a few minutes' lead, he appeared to be on foot while Norman had driven. Why was the man traveling on foot?

Inside, the building was dark. There weren't even any night lights burning. Norman could hear his heels clicking on the tile floor.

Four steps into the lobby, he stopped to let his eyes adjust to the darkness. He put the mallet back in his right hand and reached toward his open shirt with his left hand to feel for the cross. Cheryl said he was dense for refusing to accept her assessment that Pierce was both supernatural and malevolent. He still did not accept it, but standing here in the darkness he was a lot less sure of his doubt.

He decided he should start with Pierce's office. That seemed to be the center of gravity for everything that happened around here.

He felt his way across the lobby and found the elevators. He pressed the up-button, and its indicator light cast a friendly green glow into the gloom in front of the elevator doors. He heard a door slide open, and then one of the elevators appeared to be darker than the others. He went over to it and felt at the door with his mallet. It was open.

He squinted into the darkness. He thought he could see a carpeted floor inside the elevator car, but before getting in he felt around with the mallet to assure himself the car was actually present. Then he stepped in, found the fifth-floor button by feel, and pressed it.

The elevator door closed, and the car began to rise. There was no light except for the LED floor indicators that flashed above the door. After an eternity, the elevator stopped and the door rumbled open.

Norman stepped into the dark hallway. He felt his way along the wall toward Finance. When he got there, the double doors to the reception area were open. The unshaded windows along one wall of the reception area let in light from the arc lamps over the parking lot outside, filling the room with a sort of weak twilight. Norman looked around the reception area. On the other side of the room, near the door to Pierce's office, he saw a woman. He couldn't be sure, but he thought — he hoped — it might be Gwen.

"Gwen?" Norman started toward her.

"Gwen?"

She didn't answer.

When he was still about ten feet from her, Norman tripped on something and fell to the floor, dropping the mallet. The pointed end of the stake in his belt caught the inside of his thigh, and pain shot up his leg. He didn't think the stake had actually punctured the skin, but it hurt and he felt sure there would be a bruise there. Why in the world was he walking around in the dark with a pointed implement stuck in his belt? He must have lost his mind. He yanked the stake from his belt and started to throw it across the room, but stopped himself, thinking it would be crazy to throw away anything that might be useful.

He turned to see what he had tripped on. He could not make it out, but then one of the lights went on. He looked back toward Gwen and saw Pierce standing next to her with his hand on the light switch.

"Hello, Norman."

"Gwen." Norman got to his knees and started to rise.

"Believe me, Norman," said Pierce, "she's all right. She's a little groggy, but I got here in time." He gestured toward the thing Norman had tripped over.

Norman turned and saw what it was. Even if the face had not been familiar, he would have recognized the power suit, long overdue for a cleaning. Jacqueline was absolutely still, and the handle of Pierce's letter opener, the baselard, protruded from the center of her chest.

"A remarkable employee," said Pierce. "I am afraid I managed her rather badly, though."

Norman recoiled from the body.

"I don't know what you're afraid of, Norman," said Pierce. "A dead person? She's been dead for nearly a week now, and you haven't let it bother you very much. You're not what I would call one of those sensitive managers, you know. One would hope that most supervisors would take some notice of problems troubling their subordinates. But your principal subordinate has been dead for a week, and you haven't even tried to get her into the Employee Assistance Program."

Norman retrieved the croquet mallet and used it as a crutch to slowly stand, favoring his bruised leg and taking care not to stab himself with his stake again. "I've come for Gwen, Pierce."

"She has a great future ahead of her, Norman. I don't think you want to spoil it for her."

Norman knew what he had to do. He transferred the stake to his left hand again, then tossed the mallet upward by its head so he could catch it by the handle. But before he could start toward Pierce, Pierce started toward him.

Norman understood the futility of his situation. His boss had apparently run here faster than Norman had driven the same distance. How could he hope for him to stand still while Norman pounded a stake into his chest?

"I had missed my last feeding when Jacqueline came along, and I couldn't restrain myself." Pierce carried on a businesslike conversation while he walked straight toward Norman. "I have a history of that, I'm afraid."

"Don't come any closer, Pierce." Norman raised the stake with the pointed end toward Pierce and brought his mallet up behind it.

"I had thought she was going to be different. But she was like the rest — uncontrollable." Pierce walked up to Norman and grabbed the pointed end of the stake. It was still pointed at his chest. "I told her to leave Gwen alone, but she followed her home and took her right out of your house. She brought her back here to feed on her. Jacqueline felt comfortable here. The revenants often feel like that about a place." Pierce held the other end of the stake at his chest while he talked, as if daring Norman to strike it home.

With his own grip firmly on his end of the stake, Norman swung his mallet. But Pierce yanked the stake away, and it wasn't there when the mallet arrived to strike it. The mallet swished through the air toward Pierce, but it struck nothing, and Norman was thrown off balance. Norman found himself thinking the man was incredibly agile.

"I never met such an ambitious manager." Pierce

looked at the stake in his hands, shrugged, and stuck it in his belt. "I'll probably need this."

Norman recovered his balance, braced himself, and made a two-handed swing with the mallet at Pierce's head. He hit something hard enough to make the handle vibrate, but it wasn't what he was aiming at. It was the palm of Pierce's hand. Pierce had caught the head of the mallet as if Norman had lobbed him a softball. He smiled and pulled the mallet from Norman's hands.

"I'll need this, too." Pierce took a step toward Norman. "She's been all over the company. I have a plague of revenants on my hands."

Norman knew he would have to do something. Pierce was now within a step of him. He reached into his open shirt and pulled out his cross, holding it up in front of Pierce's face.

Pierce saw the cross and smiled.

"Don't come any closer," said Norman.

"Do you think this can protect you?" Pierce grabbed the dangling cross and yanked it with enough force to break the chain.

Norman felt the chain explode in his hands and heard its metal beads scatter across the room.

"This bit of iconography is so human." Pierce said "human" as if it meant "bestial."

Norman said nothing, but he was conscious of a deep fear.

"This is no protection for you, Norman." Pierce dropped the cross on the carpeting and ground it into the nap with his heel. He brought his face very close to Norman's.

"Are you going to bite me?" said Norman.

"Bite?" Pierce looked at him with puzzlement for a moment. "Oh, you mean am I going to feed on you?"

Norman just wanted to get out of there and call the police.

"No, I'm not going to feed on you. I feed only once a season, and I don't need to right now."

"Didn't you feed on Jacqueline?" said Norman.

"Yes," said Pierce. "Rather too much, I'm afraid."

"That was only days ago," said Norman. "Now it looks like you've fed on Gwen."

They both looked at Gwen, who was standing where Pierce had left her, staring into the distance.

"Just because I don't need it doesn't mean I don't want it from time to time," said Pierce. "But don't worry. You don't interest me the way your wife did earlier today."

Norman's fear gave way to annoyance. "Is there something wrong with me?"

"Of course not," said Pierce. "I just don't find you very interesting. Surely, there are some nourishing foods that you simply don't care to have. I don't care to have you."

"What's going to happen to Gwen now?" said Norman.

"I don't have any supernatural powers, and I don't enslave people. I am continually astonished with the kind of ridiculous notions you people come up with about me and my race."

Norman pointed at Gwen. "You're lying. She's like a zombie."

"No," said Pierce. "She's just tired. A feeding does that to you. But it will pass in a day or so and she'll be fine. I fed only briefly."

Norman started toward her, and Pierce did not try to stop him.

"I think I'm finally learning to control myself," said Pierce.

Norman took Gwen's hand. It was warm the way it should be. He put an arm behind her back and bent over to put the other under her knees, so he could carry her. She was heavier than he expected.

"Wha—" she said.

"It's all right." Norman staggered a step or two, then set her back down. "Just go to sleep."

He bent down, embraced her knees, and tipped her over his shoulder in a fireman's carry. She seemed nearly comatose.

"Take her home, Norman," said Pierce. "She can call me tomorrow — if she wants to. You, on the other hand, might as well stay home. I may not want to feed on you, but I have decided to terminate you."

Norman tried to hurry to get away from him.

"I'm not coming after you," said Pierce from behind him. "A century ago, I would have thought it too dangerous to let you live. But frankly, I'm getting bored. I had hoped turnaround management would be enough to engage my interest, but it hasn't turned out the way I expected."

Norman reached the elevator, and when he pressed the button the door opened immediately. He stepped inside and pressed the button for the first floor.

"Call the police if you wish," said Pierce. "Now *that* could be interesting."

The elevator door closed, and Norman was starting to feel relieved — until he realized Pierce was probably running down the stairs to meet him in the lobby and kill him. He knew now that Pierce liked to play with his food.

But Pierce wasn't in the lobby.

Norman took Gwen through the front door and out to the parking lot. He set her down and leaned her up against the car while he opened the door. Then he helped her into the car and got her seated in the passenger's seat. He walked around to his side of the car and climbed in.

"Is it time to get up?" she said.

"Go back to sleep." Norman fastened her seat belt.

But she didn't go back to sleep.

"What happened?" said Gwen.

"Jacqueline kidnapped you," said Norman.

"I was so tired and so sleepy that it seemed like a dream," said Gwen.

"Just get some rest," said Norman. "We can deal with all of this tomorrow."

Pierce had said she would be fine in a day or so, but he didn't know Gwen and her stamina. She questioned Norman about things all the way home and wanted to know why he hadn't done something about Pierce sooner.

"I didn't really know what he was," said Norman. "And he's a very decisive manager, you know. It's hard to contradict somebody like that."

Norman pulled the car into the driveway and shut off the ignition. They sat in the dark and talked.

"He expects you to call him tomorrow," said Norman.

"So he can do that to me again?" Gwen rubbed her neck. "That's bullshit."

"Don't you have—" Norman interrupted himself and tried to think of some way to phrase what he wanted to say. But he couldn't think of any way, so he just said it. "Don't you have some sort of compulsion to go back to him? Isn't it a sort of a sexual thing or something?"

"No, Norman. It's not a sexual thing. He has a sort of hypnotic technique that relaxes you so you don't feel much like resisting, but it's no more sexual than a blood test. I'm not interested in seeing him again."

Gwen was able to walk from the car under her own power, and by the time they got into the living room she seemed to be nearly at her regular energy level. Cheryl told them that the kids had never awakened, and she stared at Norman with frank admiration.

"You did it, Norman!" said Cheryl. "You rescued her!"

Norman didn't feel he had really rescued anybody, but he noticed Gwen was looking at him differently.

Cheryl wanted to stay and plan strategy for dealing with Pierce, but Norman told her to go home and walked her to the door. There wasn't any way to "deal with"

Pierce. He intended to call the police and tell them about Jacqueline, but he suspected that if the police were any danger to Pierce, he would be long gone before they arrived. Right now, all he wanted to do was get some rest and in the morning work on updating his resume.

"Let's get ready for bed," he said to Gwen.

But she was looking at him in a way she never had before. "You risked a lot to come get me."

"I figured it was either that or lose you," he said.

She smiled. "Do you want to get a shower with me?"

EIGHTEEN

PIERCE watched Norman and Gwen leave, then he laid the croquet mallet and stake on a nearby desk, switched off the light, and walked over to Jacqueline's body to retrieve the baselard. He grasped the handle and pulled it from her chest. She had not had the chance to feed on Gwen and didn't bleed very much.

He looked down at the baselard in his hand. A sheen of dark liquid covered the blade, and the face on the handle's pommel glistened with a bit of the parking lot arc lamps outside the window. The blade was a little longer than necessary for opening mail, but he was glad he'd kept it here in the office. The baselard was a wonderful instrument, evocative of the eighteenth century in which it was made.

Pierce traveled light, but the few things he owned generally came from the eighteenth century. He had fond memories of that time and liked to keep a connection with it. The baselard was so much like that time: functional, well-balanced, easy and comfortable to handle, decorated like a wedding cake.

People went out of their way with decoration in those days, but by and large the world made sense then. In those days, work consisted of making things. That certainly was no longer the case, but what had happened?

He reached into his pocket, took out a handkerchief, and wiped the blade of the baselard with it. It would be hours before there would be any people in the building, and he had plenty of time to decide about Jacqueline's body. He walked back into his office, stepping carefully over a lab technician who was lying in the doorway with a hole, very much like the one Jacqueline had, in his chest.

Pierce went and sat at the desk, wondering how many more revenants he might have to take care of. He hadn't had time to question Jacqueline about how many times she'd fed. There had been a fight when he caught her with Gwen. Jacqueline was surprisingly powerful, but she had no experience dealing with anyone like Pierce.

It was not an emotion he felt used to, but Pierce was sorry about Jacqueline. He could have fed lightly on her and she would still be alive and productive.

It really was too bad, too, because he would probably need her for this marketing database thing. It was a good idea, but Pierce had begun to realize he didn't trust it. He was, in fact, deeply suspicious of the very company he was engaged in turning around. Every company is unique, but Biomethods, Inc. was the strangest place Pierce had ever worked. All these employees, all these resources, and they didn't even make anything. To the extent the company had a business at all (and it was difficult to find amid all the overhead activities), it consisted of licensing discoveries.

They didn't produce anything here but information. Some of the scientists didn't even work with animals, but did all their experiments on computer models. They took information and manipulated it in various ways and then counted those manipulations as their output.

Nobody was making anything here. There was no plant, no big machines, no raw materials. And it was so quiet all the time! It was less like a business than a library.

Pierce thought about the factories he had built, the assembly lines he had designed, the manufacturing processes he had engineered. And he realized he felt out of place at Biomethods. Indeed, he felt out of place in this decade.

Had he learned anything here?

A picture of Norman leaving with Gwen flashed into his mind.

Only that one cannot make a border collie out of a sheep.

Floyd Kemske is the author of *The Virtual Boss* (Catbird, 1993) and *Lifetime Employment* (Catbird, 1992). He lives in Pepperell, Massachusetts.